The Party

Also by Tessa Hadley

The Party

Tessa Hadley

JONATHAN CAPE
LONDON

1 3 5 7 9 10 8 6 4 2

Jonathan Cape, an imprint of Vintage, is part of the
Penguin Random House group of companies whose addresses
can be found at global.penguinrandomhouse.com

First published by Jonathan Cape in 2024

penguin.co.uk/vintage

Typeset in 11.5/16.5pt Stempel Garamond LT Std
by Jouve (UK), Milton Keynes
Printed and bound in Great Britain by Clays Ltd, Elcograf S.p.A.

The authorised representative in the EEA is
Penguin Random House Ireland, Morrison Chambers,
32 Nassau Street, Dublin D02 YH68

A CIP catalogue record for this book is available from
the British Library

ISBN 9781787335554

Penguin Random House is committed to a sustainable future for our
business, our readers and our planet. This book is made from Forest
Stewardship Council® certified paper.

for Gilly

and for the Happy Cranes
Tom, Tim and Jenny

1

Vincent's Party

The party was in full swing. Evelyn could hear the sexy blare of the trad jazz almost as soon as she got off the bus at St Mary Redcliffe and began walking over to the Steam Packet, the pub which Vincent – who was a friend of Evelyn's older sister Moira – had commandeered for that evening. He'd decided they all needed a party to cheer them up, because the winter had been so bitter, and because now in February the incessant rain had turned the snow to slush. It was raining again this evening; the bus's wiper had beaten its numb rhythm all the way into town, the pavements were dark with wet, the gutters ran with water. Frozen filthy formless lumps, the remainders of the snow, persisted at the street corners and in the deep recesses between the buildings, loomed sinisterly in the gaping bombsites. Crossing the road, Evelyn had to put up her umbrella – actually her mother's worn old green umbrella with the broken rib and the duck's head handle, which she'd borrowed without asking on her way out, because she'd lost her own somewhere. Probably she'd get in trouble for this tomorrow, but she didn't care, she was too full of agitated happiness. Anything could happen between now and tomorrow. Evelyn couldn't believe her luck, that she was going to an actual party – and not just any dull ordinary party but this wild one with her sister's friends, in a half-derelict old pub with a terrible reputation, hanging over the black water in the city docks. If her parents had known where the party was they'd never have let her out, but she'd lied to them so fluently and easily, saying that Moira had promised to look after her, and that they were meeting in the Victoria Rooms. She was proud of herself. Who knew that you could be a Sunday school teacher one minute, asking the children to crayon in pictures of Jesus holding up a lantern, with a lost lamb tucked under his other arm, and then lie to your parents with such perfectly calibrated innocent sweetness?

The rain didn't matter, Evelyn was impervious to it. Picking her way between the streams of water rippling on the roads, not wanting to spoil her fashionable unsuitable black ballet flats, she enjoyed the contrast between this desolate outer universe and the heat of her life burning up inside. When she'd had to change buses at the Centre, she'd gone into a cubicle in the

Ladies public toilets to take off her wellington boots, and also the decent wool dress she'd put on over her actual party clothes, so that her parents couldn't see what she was wearing: skin-tight black slacks zipped up along the insides of her calves, black polo-neck jumper, wide red leather belt with a black buckle. Evelyn was very thin, with a long neck – a swan neck, she thought – and flat stomach, jutting hip bones; she hoped that she looked spectacular, hair scraped back from her face like a dancer's and breasts thrust up in a new brassiere. She longed for and feared the moment when she would shed her thick winter coat and reveal herself. To tell the truth she feared everything: part of her wanted to get straight back on the 28 bus and go home. Peering at her reflection in the square of tin which served as a mirror above the sink in the Ladies toilet, she had clipped huge false pearls on her ears – those were her mother's too – and painted her mouth stickily with red lipstick. The boots and the dress were bundled now into a shopping bag which she'd have to jettison somewhere, along with her coat and the umbrella, for collection later.

The Steam Packet's austere broad silhouette, three storeys tall, was stark against the gaps the bombing had left in the skyline: rows of windows in the upper storeys of its facade were lightless or boarded up, but a yellowish light shone enticingly from the ground floor. A clamour of raised voices drew Evelyn toward it, her body beginning to move already to the music. As far as she was concerned this old Bristol pub could have been on the dockside somewhere in New Orleans, about which she had indefinite but potent ideas. Moira hadn't promised to look after her. In fact Moira didn't even know that she was coming to the party, and probably wouldn't want her there, but Evelyn was desperate to be part of her sister's crowd. The girls were born two years apart; Moira complained about her kid sister always tagging along after her friends, just as she used to complain when they were children. Evelyn had usually tagged along anyway, when they were turned out from the house to fend for themselves for the day, Moira jolting their baby brother along in the pram and intent on some mission with her gang, rolling up leaves in cigarette papers to smoke them, or climbing onto the roof of the glasshouse in the park, or spying on their neighbour who'd lost his mind and walked around nude in the garden.

It was Vincent who'd invited Evelyn to the party, last week when she'd bumped into him in Queens Road on her way to a lecture, and he told her he'd persuaded the landlord of the Packet to let him take the place over for an evening. Vincent knew everyone: not just the arty people, although he was an art student like Moira, but also taxi drivers and bookies and chip-shop owners, pub landlords and veteran soldiers missing limbs from the first war; he talked to these characters for hours and learned their stories, snatching them in clever charcoal drawings in his sketchbook. He paid court to a toothless old woman who ran a second-hand clothes shop, where garments were heaped in a rotting dark mulch against the window glass; you could see the moths and the fleas jumping out, Moira said, from between the layers of clothes. This old woman would save certain items for Vincent, so that he came to classes dressed in an airman's leather jacket or an evening cloak lined in red satin; Moira refused to sit near him then, because of the fleas and because the old clothes stank of naphthalene from the mothballs. Vincent was tall, with eager moist brown eyes, a booming voice, and a lot of chestnut-brown curly hair. He wore a wide-brimmed soft black felt hat like Augustus John and played in a jug band.

—Vincent's very good-looking, Evelyn had said experimentally to Moira once, when Moira was cutting out a skirt pinned with a paper pattern on the dining-room table at home, crunching her scissors confidently through the fabric which parted so cleanly in their wake. She was studying fashion at college, and could do tailoring like a professional.

—Ye-es.

—What do you mean, ye-es?

—Shush, Evelyn, let me concentrate. I don't know: he's got all the ingredients but somehow he isn't attractive. Not to me at any rate.

Moira's discriminations were subtle and absolute.

Evelyn dropped her voice, so that their mother couldn't hear from the kitchen. —Is he queer?

—God, no. Don't be an idiot.

—Well *I* don't know. I've never known anyone who *was* queer.

—You've known loads of them, only you never noticed it. Half of the awful old spinsters who taught at our school, for instance. But not Vince. Vince tries to get off with everyone. He'll probably try with you. You'd better watch out. Unless you do find him attractive, of course.

—No, I don't think I do, Evelyn said.

How could she find him attractive, after Moira had said he wasn't? —I know what you mean. He's sort of woolly somehow.

Moira laughed, in spite of herself. —*Woolly?*

—Yes: like a fuzzy old favourite toy or something. A teddy bear with big glassy eyes.

—Well he's not *my* favourite toy.

—Nor my favourite either, Evelyn said thoughtfully.

* * *

The public bar in the Steam Packet was already full, with the band squeezed into a corner blasting out music, and everyone shouting to be heard over them. The place was dimly lit by bare electric bulbs,

8

dangling from loops of wire festooned along the old beams; Vincent explained delightedly that the pub hadn't been connected to mains electricity since the war, they were just piggy-backing off someone else's supply. A few couples were dancing already, in a tight space where the tables had been pushed back; there was sawdust on the stone-flagged floor, the rough-hewn benches and tables and three-legged stools were scarred and gouged, and the plaster walls – stained a dark mahogany colour from tobacco smoke – were crowded with advertising for brands of beer and rum and pipe tobacco which hadn't existed for decades, alongside paintings and photographs of ships, and model ships in glass bottles thick with dust, set on blue-painted frozen choppy seas. A chunk of tree smouldered sulkily to ash in a dirty open hearth at the far end of the room. The young people by this time were generating their own heat.

Vincent was officiating behind the bar, where a few sticky bottles were reflected in ornate mirror-glass; he was ladling out cider from an open tin bucket, and the pub landlord – wizened and tiny as a jockey, with blue eyes clear as chips of ice and a face wrinkled into folds like a chestnut – was sitting on a bar stool in front of it, overseeing things sceptically. He didn't drink the cider himself, apparently, but preferred neat gin – Hollands, he called it; Vincent said he was pickled in it. Some of the rough-looking men standing up at the bar must be his regular customers: it was a dockers' pub, Vincent had said, where prostitutes came to find customers. Evelyn had never seen prostitutes but she'd read about them in novels. It was a big thing among the art students, to want to mingle across those boundaries of class their parents were so intent upon policing: their mothers putting doilies on the cake-plate as if respectability depended upon it, objecting to milk or ketchup bottles on the table, ironing handkerchiefs and socks and dusters. Many of the students hadn't come far from the working class themselves; Vincent's dad was a plumber in Ashley Down. Moira and Evelyn's maternal grandfather was a coal miner – and yet their father was petitioning to join the Masons. After the war he'd got a job with the Port of Bristol Authority, and they'd moved down to Avonmouth from the north-east of England, leaving their history behind, and a whole tribe of aunts and uncles and cousins on their mother's side.

—Oh it's you, Moira remarked without enthusiasm when Evelyn had stowed her coat, and the bag with her boots and dress and umbrella, under a table in one corner which was a makeshift cloakroom. Moira absorbed her sister's outfit in one scouring, appraising glance. —Looks nice, she said, grudging but fair. Evelyn was wondering now, however, whether her Left Bank-themed black clothes might have been the wrong choice for the Packet. Moira was wearing her striped full skirt and a cream blouse; someone had told her once that you should aim to make other women in the room look overdressed. That was the difference between them, Evelyn thought. She would go for something striking and zany, which might work and might not, while Moira would never be so foolish as to take that risk. Evelyn veered between two extremes: either she spent hours dressing herself up extravagantly, or she slopped around at home in her oldest scruffy skirt and cardigan and slippers. Her scruffy self was her reading self. To lose herself properly in a book she had to be crumpled and snug, oblivious of her appearance, scrunched up in an armchair with her shoes off and her legs tucked under her. When she was really reading, she forgot who she was. Yet when she went out to lectures or classes – she was in her first year studying French at the university – she dressed up anxiously in front of the mirror, to make herself look more like a student and an intellectual: beret tilted to one side, silk scarf fastened insouciantly around her throat. *Insouciante*, she murmured with a French accent, gazing adoringly at herself, finishing off her outfit with a couple of books under her arm.

The two sisters weren't completely unalike in their appearance. There was a family stamp on both of them, and on their younger brother: they were all strong-featured, full-lipped, dark-browed, with a long doleful nose the girls hated, although actually it made their faces more interesting. The nose came from their father, who was handsome and stern: it was all right on a man, a war hero, first lieutenant on an aircraft carrier that had escorted merchant convoys across the Atlantic. Both sisters were good-looking, although Moira insisted she wasn't, she just knew how to make the best of herself.

—I look more like *him*, Moira said. —You're the lucky one.

Their mother had pretty dark soft Irish looks, although she'd let herself go and grown shapeless, because she was unhappy in the south and in her marriage. Moira was always telling her off for slouching, or eating too much starch; meanwhile Moira was critical of her own defects too, staring them down, calculating and resigned. —I hate these lumps of fat under my arms. These I do have from Mam.

Whenever she and Evelyn went out together though, it was Moira the men were drawn to, with her self-possession and sophisticated allure; beside her Evelyn felt girlish and gauche, however hard she tried. —You shouldn't talk too much, Moira advised unhelpfully. —Don't talk right in their faces.

—What lumps of fat? asked Evelyn, lifting up her arms and screwing her neck round to look for lumps.

—*These* ones. You don't even have them, they're

hideous. If I had the money I'd have them cut out. And I'd have my nose shortened. Film stars do it.

*   *   *

At Vincent's party, however, Moira had that dreamily smiling, assured look she wore in public, attention only brushing gauzily against the present moment around her. And she'd managed to get a table in just the right position – not so near the band that conversation was difficult, but commanding a good view. She was sitting with Josephine LaPalma and two men Evelyn had never seen before. Josephine modelled at the art college and was one of Vincent's characters, glamorous and dangerous, with a broad Bristol accent – it was a coup for him that he'd persuaded her to come. She was supposed to have gypsy blood, and her black hair reached down to her waist when she undid it; it was wound tonight in a thick plait around her head. Everything about Josephine fitted in with the students' romantic idea of a bohemian life. She was even having an affair with a married man, one of the teachers at the college, a talented painter.

The two men looked keenly at Evelyn as she joined the table, and stood up to be introduced, as if they belonged somewhere more formal; the older one bent over the hand she held out, to kiss it. They fussed about getting her a chair until she said she could just

13

squeeze onto the bench with Moira – *oho, slumming it*, they cried. Their names were Paul and something she didn't quite catch, like Sandy or Simon. These men's clothes and their voices and demeanour weren't quite right for Vincent's party: too conventional, something artificial and sneering barely concealed under the sugary surface. Even Evelyn could see that their clothes were expensive, made from fine cloth, and the one who kissed her hand smelled of some subtle cologne. They behaved with that mixture of assurance and awkwardness which was a sign of certain types, privileged and posh. In the crowd jostling around them the women wore peasant skirts and striped sailors' tops – none of the men, apart from these two, were wearing ties. Evelyn couldn't help sneaking glances, though, at the younger man at their table, Paul, who didn't talk as much as his friend, and looked as if he might be quite drunk already. His movements and his speech were slow and syrupy and he smiled privately, communing with himself, brilliantined treacle-coloured hair flopping across his forehead, blinking eyes and dimpled chin making him seem sleepy and childlike. His perfect features were like an angel's in a picture: upper lip very full, the curve of his cheek like a peach. He might be corrupted, Evelyn thought, remembering some of the poetry she knew.

Paul insisted on buying Evelyn a drink: she said she'd have a gin and orange. She hadn't really learned to like the taste of alcohol yet, she only liked its effects. The older man thought she was very wise.

—The cider's undrinkable. We think that creatures have drowned in it.

—Oh, they *encourage* creatures to drown in it. Everything adds to the flavour, Moira assured them solemnly. She and Josephine were drinking the cider laced with blackcurrant, to make it palatable – most of the students did that.

—Well Evelyn, the older man asked, —are you an art student as well?

She told them she wasn't, that she was studying French.

—French? *La Belle Dame Sans Merci!* Gosh, what brainy girls you all are. I'm perfectly terrified.

Josephine reassured him languorously. —You needn't worry. I'm an absolute idiot.

—You don't look like an idiot to me, he said. —I expect you know which side your bread's buttered on.

—She isn't an idiot, Evelyn said. —The artists all want to paint her.

—I'll bet they do. I suppose they pay you to model, do they?

—Nobody works for free.

—Clothes on, or off?

He wasn't looking at Josephine as he asked this, but grinning at Paul.

Josephine was indifferent. —Mostly off.

—I wouldn't let any daughter of mine earn money that way.

She laughed at him. —Your daughter might be too ugly. Maybe they wouldn't want to paint her.

This older man had springy pale hair and rubbery froggy features; his manicured hands – collecting up glasses or reaching his lighter to their cigarettes, gold signet ring on one stubby finger – made Evelyn think of that conjuring trick, where you moved coloured pots around so fast that no one could guess where the bean was hidden. Under cover of his attention to her and Moira, Evelyn saw, he was more fascinated by Josephine. He spoke to her differently – jeering and presumptuous and yet afraid of her. —Vincent's besotted with Josephine, Evelyn insisted. —He's painted and drawn her over and over a thousand times, but she's not interested in him. Great artists often marry their models, you know.

Josephine protested, serene in herself, blowing smoke rings. —Shut up exaggerating. Vince says those things to everyone.

The man said that they didn't know anyone at the party, they'd never met Vincent before; he'd bumped into them outside on the street and persuaded them to come in. —So you have to take pity on us and look after us, he said, in a tone of wheedling teasing flirtation. Evelyn decided that these two men didn't care anything about art or literature, and she wished that

16

Vincent hadn't invited them; yet Moira was energised and spiky, as if she enjoyed their sparring. Mostly she was talking to the older one, but of course her attention was really on the beautiful boy Paul, who rested his chin on his fist and stared into his drink. The older man's name was Sinden, it turned out: which was his surname. He didn't like his Christian name, he explained, and wouldn't tell them what it was, however much they begged him. —I can't believe the things women get interested in, he complained. —Now a man wouldn't care less about my Christian name, once I said I wasn't using it. What does it matter, something my mother chose at a time when I didn't have any say in the matter? I wouldn't trust her to name a dog of mine.

Moira appealed to Paul. —What is it though, what is his name?

—I don't know, Christ knows, who cares, Paul laughed. —He's just Sinden.

—But imagine if there weren't any women in the world though, Evelyn said.

Sinden pretended he was anguished by that idea, grabbing at her hand and pressing it against his shirt-front to make her feel his heart beat faster; the material of his white shirt was clammy from his body heat, slippery against the vest he wore underneath. He groaned suggestively. —No women! Alas, alack! What would we do without them? But I'll let you in on a little secret, Evelyn: it isn't your curiosity we adore you for. What is it makes us put up with all your nonsense?

—But no: seriously imagine it, Evelyn persisted, trying to have a proper conversation. —No one would find anything out if there were no women asking questions. No one would know anything apart from the surface things. All the secrets would just rot away unnoticed, there would just be a sort of empty framework left. Like one of those wire things they build up plaster on. An armature.

—I love a bit of gossip, Josephine said. —Keeps the world going round.

Sinden winked at her. —It isn't gossip keeps it going round.

—You think it's money then? Or sex?

—That's a poser for you, Sinden, said Paul, lifting his head from his drink. —Money or sex, old chap?

—Depends what time of day, Sinden said. —Depends how many drinks I've had.

—You need the money first, Paul said. —To buy the drinks that make you think that you don't care about the money.

Sinden beckoned them in confidentially, speaking in a hoarse whisper; Evelyn moved her knees away from his under the table. —My friend here has got plenty of it, too, he said. —Money coming out of Paul's ears, doesn't need to do a day's work in his life.

You should see the fine old car we have parked around the corner. Let's just say that once upon a time his family were in the tobacco industry, and when they sold, they invested the proceeds wisely.

Listening to this description of his wealth, Paul looked bashful and complacent, almost coy. Sinden told them that Paul had been giving him a tour of the war damage: he'd never been to Bristol before. —I'm a friend of his older brother Tommy, he and I were at school together. But we've left Tommy at home, he says he isn't well. Doesn't know what he's missing! Little did we know we were going to bump into you girls! Claims he's got influenza but we think he's making a fuss and it's just a common or garden old cold, don't we, Paul?

—Dreadful hypochondriac, my brother.

—So Paul's been showing me round and I'm convinced there are opportunities here. For the right sort of people. A fresh start for the city. Building for the future.

—Do you know about building then? Moira asked. —Is that what you do?

—I'm not a builder, he laughed. —Do I look like a builder? But I do have very good contacts, with the right sort of men who have the right sort of friends. Contacts are the important thing.

—Sounds like profiteering to me, Josephine said. —I hate profiteering.

—And what's wrong with making a nice clean profit, out of something everybody wants? That way we win all round.

—They should just cut out the middleman. Then everything in this city would be a damn sight cheaper. Building by the people, for the people.

—She's a Red! Sinden exclaimed delightedly, staring at her with his goggle eyes.

—And so what if I am?

—I've never met a real live Red before! Seen a few dead ones . . .

—Take a good look, Josephine said. —Looking is free.

She settled herself at ease as if she were posing, presenting her head in its dramatic profile, rugged and magnificent as a ship's figurehead. Sinden couldn't believe, he said, staring at her, how three such lovely girls hadn't been snapped up. How come they weren't any of them wearing engagement rings? Weren't there any red-blooded men around here? —Moira is engaged, Evelyn blurted out, as if she were defending their honour, or Moira's honour at least. —Sort of engaged. Her boyfriend's gone as a policeman to Malaya.

—Cass isn't my boyfriend.

—Christ, the poor sap, Sinden said.

Evelyn protested, astonished. —Why a poor sap?

—I doubt if you'll see him again.

—But we will see him!

—Don't suppose he speaks a word of Chinese. I know that game. Put him in charge of a squad of men he can't talk to, armed with weapons he doesn't know how to use, in a terrain he doesn't understand. They'll supply him with some soft-skinned Austin or Land Rover. Done for at the first road ambush, driving between the plantations he's supposed to be protecting.

—But how do you know all that?

He tapped the side of his nose. —I know what I know.

—And why are you gloating? It sounds as if you're glad that he might die.

Sinden's horrible knowingness was hard and irrefutable as a rock, Evelyn thought. You couldn't push back against it unless you understood about guns and vehicles and politics, all those brutally real things. It didn't make any difference that you knew reams of French poetry: *un trouble s'éleva dans mon âme éperdue*, or *je plongerai ma tête amoureuse d'ivresse*.

Moira stared dry-eyed at Sinden, challenging him to find the least sign that she cared. —Cass wasn't my boyfriend. I told him not to go. I knew it was stupid. We never were engaged. He went on about this cash bonus they were offering, at the end of one year.

—Good luck with that, he scoffed. —Getting through to the end of a year.

—Risking his neck, Paul said, stirring to wakefulness

21

and slurring his words, —when he could have been spending the evening here with you.

—You see: Paul likes you, Sinden said triumphantly. —I knew that he would. He's pretty choosy, our friend Paul, but he likes you, Moira. Now why don't you two lovebirds get dancing, while I buy us more drinks?

Josephine said that she was leaving, going on to another party; Evelyn didn't want anything, she hadn't finished her first gin and orange. The band was playing a bluesy number and as Paul stood up from the table he pretended to be parping along on an imaginary slide trombone, as if the music were a comedy laid on for his benefit; Sinden joined in on an imaginary snare drum, screwing up his face to feel the beat. Evelyn was buffeted by a gust of rage at their obliviousness. Didn't they know that this music was serious, it came out of suffering, it wasn't a game? The student crowd were all jazz enthusiasts, worshipping Louis Armstrong and Buddy Bolden and King Oliver, whose lives and art set a high-water mark for everything tragic and joyous; the musicians in the band were just white Bristolians, but seemed to borrow some of that glamour. There were a couple of coloured men drinking at the bar: they weren't art students of course, but must be pub regulars from the docks. The students approached them and spoke to them with wary respect.

Evelyn thought Moira might refuse to dance, if she

was upset by how Sinden had spoken about Cass. But she moved suavely enough into Paul's arms, with that remote vague look as if she hardly saw him. Paul wasn't tall but he wasn't slight like a boy: he was muscled and substantial, more authoritative now that he was on his feet. When they'd squeezed their way among the couples on the dance floor, he let his head droop onto Moira's shoulder and his body rested against hers heavily, as if he really was drunk. He danced well, though, responding after all to the music's sluggish melancholy. Evelyn had the surprising thought that bodies were sometimes wiser than the people inside them. She'd have liked to impress somebody with this idea, but couldn't explain it to Sinden, who would misunderstand her deliberately. When she saw Paul rouse and lift his head to say something in Moira's ear, pulling her closer with his slow smile and sleepy eyes, Evelyn was stricken with envious desire, in spite of everything. Whatever he said ignited some response in Moira, so that she smiled back secretively, pretending to reproach him, pushing him off a little, cautious as ever, not giving anything away. Evelyn had a horror then of Sinden asking her to dance out of sheer obligation, taking second best. She didn't want to dance with him anyway, she didn't like him. So when he got up to go to the bar she made her escape with Josephine, said she was popping outside for a bit of air.

—Don't fall in the water, Sinden said. —It's dark out there.

*　*　*

Emerging so abruptly, out of the noise and heat of the pub, into the night's blackness and wetness and quiet, Evelyn wondered for a moment if she was drunk: but that didn't seem likely after just one gin. —Don't men just like to talk? Josephine said. —They love the sound of their own voices.

Then she hurried away, her big coat flapping, head down in her gypsy scarf, heels clacking on the pavement, resounding on the metal footbridge, weaving among the shadowy, slouching men, not afraid of walking all by herself through the docklands. It wasn't quite dark: there were street lamps on the road and lights on some of the wharves and in the timber yards. Light seeped from the pub windows onto its forecourt, where the cobbles gleamed with wet although it had stopped raining; beyond this forecourt a wall dropped abruptly to the water ten foot below in a narrow channel, cut through from the Floating Harbour into the Basin. On summer nights couples would sit swinging their legs on the wall, drinking the lethal Kingston Black cider, but in winter the idea of that enclosed invisible water was furtive and chilly. When something splashed in the blackness,

Evelyn thought of rats. A call from one of the ships in the Basin, in no language she recognised, bounced eerily along the surface of the water.

Probably there wasn't really any other party, she thought; probably Josephine was hurrying to meet her lover, the married artist. Then she felt sick with loneliness: she longed for a lover of her own and was ashamed of her inexperience, her poor judgement. Things had been hopeless when she was still a schoolgirl, but she'd thought something must happen now that she'd started at the university – where surely she would thrive, because she was clever. She'd imagined herself surrounded by admirers, and had even been afraid that she'd settle too easily, for someone who wasn't good enough. Evelyn could have loved Moira's Cass, for instance, Robert Cassidy, although she didn't know him well, she'd only met him a few times, when Moira allowed her to come to the pub with her crowd. Moira kept her emotional life strictly apart from her family, and their parents weren't to be told that she and Cass were engaged – and anyhow, now apparently they weren't. Yet he'd seemed fairly enthralling to Evelyn: talented, popular, a burly freckled red-headed rugby player, his blue eyes watchful and wary. He was a joker and a tease, with a gift for drawing caricatures of his friends. Since Cass had gone off to Malaya, Evelyn had loyally taken a great interest in the Emergency, looking out for snippets about it in the newspapers. It was called an Emergency, their father said, because if they called it a war then the plantation owners wouldn't be covered by their insurance.

It was too cold outside; Evelyn had only come out, anyway, to get away from where she was stuck in that corner. She needed another drink to give her the courage for throwing herself back into a party where she barely knew anyone, and no one was interested in her. A character in a novel, in her situation, would break in on conversations and introduce herself, be revealed as charming and brilliant; people would be amazed by her ideas and her sex appeal, her stylish gamine haircut. Just as Evelyn was imagining this, she heard someone come out from the pub entrance behind her and say hello. It was Donald from her French class at the university. When Vincent invited her to the party, she'd been on her way to meet Donald in Carwardine's for coffee – they were going to go over some ideas about Racine's *Phèdre*. Evelyn had passed the invitation on, wanting to impress Donald with her bold sociability, mingling with the rough life in the docks, but hadn't imagined that he'd dare to come. He was wearing the same unsuitable old striped blazer that he wore to classes.

—Are you having a good time? he said.

—Isn't this just an amazing place? Very *Fleurs du Mal*.

—Is that the name of the cider?

—Oh dear, did you drink it? I should have warned you, you need to put blackcurrant in, to take the taste away. Was it very awful?

—Definitely the worst thing I've ever drunk. No, that's not true. My brother and I made a mixture, when we were boys, one morning before anyone else was awake. I can't tell you what we put into it, because it's unseemly. I mean, along with the potato peelings from the bin, and cigarette ash and dregs from our parents' party. Then he made me drink it.

—My brother likes making evil mixtures too. He's good at chemistry.

—Come to think of it, our mixture tasted pretty similar to that cider: marginally more palatable perhaps. You look stunning, by the way. I'd drink the cider bucket dry, it goes without saying, for the chance of spending an evening with you. The sort of ordeal knights undergo in the old stories.

—I never heard of one drinking a bucket of cider.

—They always give girls the expurgated version.

Evelyn liked Donald but – it was just her luck – he was hopeless, he wouldn't do for a boyfriend. He only looked about sixteen, to start with: over-eager and stumbling and pallid, with sticking-out ears and a tense, lumpy jaw. He'd been a boarder at Queen Elizabeth's Hospital, where the boys' uniform came from history, a sort of long dress buttoning up the front, with yellow stockings and black shoes. Evelyn had seen these boys tormented in the street by children from the local schools, and once she knew that Donald had worn the yellow stockings, couldn't help imagining him in them. When Moira met him she'd said he was really sweet, pity he was so NPA, which meant Non-Physically-Attractive. Donald took off his blazer when Evelyn shivered, and put it around her shoulders. —You should come here in the summer, she encouraged him. —In the summer you can sit out on the dock.

—I should think people fall in though. After a pint or two of *Fleurs du Mal*.

—Are you drunk, Don? I don't think I've ever seen you when you're drunk. I wonder what you're like?

—I'm very adorable apparently.

—Do you feel drunk now?

He frowned, as if testing himself inwardly. —Drunk enough to fall in the water, not drunk enough to risk going anywhere near it. It's an odd kind of drunkenness, different to beer, lighter and more extreme: as if someone's just sliced off the top of my mind, like taking the top off an egg. Yet ask me to supply the past historic first-person plural of the verb *saisir*, and I bet I could still do it.

—*Nous saisîmes*, of course, you oaf.

He sighed and complained she was too quick for him; Evelyn asked him what he thought about Malaya.

—What about Malaya? I'm pretty drunk, remember. How did we get to Malaya?

—The Emergency.

—Oh, *that.* Well naturally I'm on the side of the insurgents. Down with the filthy British Empire and the filthy rubber barons and the running dogs of capitalism and so on.

—Do you really mean it?

—Cross my heart and hope to die. I mean it absolutely.

—Don't say hope to die. It might be bad luck for someone. But I'm on the same side too. I agree with you. I hate war. I hate the expression that comes on men's faces when they talk about war. Not on your face though.

—What kind of expression is it?

Evelyn had to close her eyes for a moment to conjure up Sinden precisely. —Sly, it's sly. As if they're sharing an awful dirty joke together, flicking it across in front of your eyes to tease you, but too fast for you to know what the joke is. Concupiscence in it somewhere.

—Concupiscence?

—I don't even know if that's how you pronounce it. I've never said the word out loud before.

—Definitely a word that exists primarily unspoken. But sounded pretty good to me.

—Incidentally my dad's expression isn't at all the

same, although he was actually in the war. I don't like his expression much either but it's more grown-up, like a shutter coming down. Keeping you out because you're not worthy, you're too trivial.

—I can see the concupiscence exactly. I know just what you mean. And the shutter as well. My father's a bit like that too – the shutter and the unworthiness – about most things. Though not particularly the war, which he spent in a comfortable office.

Evelyn shuddered inside the blazer's warmth and Donald put an arm tentatively around her shoulders. —Don, if we went back inside, she said, —would you buy me a drink? Because I need a boost. I'm not really enjoying myself much at this party. I'm not talking to anybody, or not anybody I actually like – I mean, apart from you of course. I'm always disappointed at parties. I long to be, you know, a *succès fou*, but I never am.

—You're a *succès fou* with me, he said.

—Yes, she said with a flare of irritation. —But that's not enough, is it?

—I suppose not.

* * *

Donald bought Evelyn a gin and orange with double gin in it, and after that the party went much better. She wasn't exactly a *succès fou*, but she submerged herself effectively in the flamboyant, quarrelsome, ecstatic, flirting mass, drifting between different groups as if she were always on her way somewhere else, telling everyone she was Moira's sister and was doing French at university, then moving off again before they could get tired of her. More drinks were bought for her from time to time, by one man or another; she danced with a couple of these men. In lieu of a lover, she decided to be in love with the glorious sinuous blasting shameless music, and with the whole jazz band collectively, from the droopy-faced ironic pianist wreathed in his cigar smoke, to the grinning drummer perched so tautly and eagerly upright on his stool; she even included the moody trumpet player, whip-thin, quiff of his thick black hair oiled like a pelt, who glared at her when she said something loudly, by mistake, over his solo in 'West End Blues'. She danced with Donald only once: predictably he was a hopeless dancer, with no sense of rhythm. —Are you actually *counting*? she accused him.

—I thought that was what you were supposed to do.

—Only when you're learning. Afterwards you've got to just feel it, in your limbs.

—I apologise for my unfeeling limbs, he said.

—And the counting's supposed to relate to the beat of the music, it's not just something random ticking over inside your own head.

—Sorry.

Evelyn introduced him to Vincent, who'd yielded his place behind the bar and was drawing excitedly in charcoal in his sketchbook. A craggy-faced man in a voluminous drab coat, monumentally patient, sat for his portrait: Vincent told them that he was a Pill pilot named Craddy, and the man croaked something hoarsely about *hobblers* and *Hung Road* and *tidal range*, which might have been intended for Donald. He hardly seemed to see Evelyn. —Did you know that the Bristol pilots and westernmen have come from Crockerne Pill since the fifteenth century? Vincent exclaimed. —A tradition handed down through the generations.

—I were 'prenticed, Craddy growled out, as if this were momentous news, —on the gaff-rigged old skiffs. Those were the days.

Evelyn's father would have known how to talk to such a man and share expertise with him: he knew all the pilots working in the Channel. She considered remarking that her father worked for the Port Authority, but thought better of it; the man didn't seem to want to look at her, and for some reason she felt ashamed for the first time that evening – in the presence of this authentic individual from the working classes – of her tight-fitting outfit, flaunting her figure. It was easier for a man to move between these worlds: arguing about cubism one minute, talking to someone like Craddy the next. Vincent was obsessed with the old life of the city, he drew it whenever he could, as if he must make a record while it lasted: Moira called his work the old rag-and-bone shop. Everything solid and particular would disappear in time, Vincent said. And so he drew the men unloading timber from the ships in the city docks, carrying the long planks on their shoulders; he drew the live giraffe they drove in a crate, on the back of a lorry, up to the zoo on the Downs; he drew the bomb damage, the broken-toothed skyline and the rain-washed exposed domesticity and intimacy of house-sides whose rooms had been torn away, the flapping ripped wallpaper and cheerless fireplaces and doors opening onto nothingness. There was a fanatic's restlessness in Vincent. He was exuberantly friendly with everyone, but never gave anyone his whole attention for long, unless he was drawing them. Which might have been why Evelyn agreed with Moira, finally, that he wasn't quite attractive, in spite of his good looks and his lovely hat.

*   *   *

Evelyn didn't lose sight of her sister, in her circulation around the party. Moira hadn't stuck with those two men, thank goodness, she'd shaken them off and danced with different people, she'd been at the heart of the knots of fun and laughter that Evelyn had most wanted to break into. Was there someone who'd replaced Robert Cassidy in Moira's affections? Evelyn kept a lookout, but couldn't see anything obvious. Towards the end of the evening, when Evelyn was thinking she needed to leave, to catch the last bus home to Avonmouth, she made her way to where Moira was standing: talking again, as it happened, to Sinden and Paul, who had their coats on and their hats in their hands. Evelyn didn't know whether Moira was coming home with her or not: often she stayed over in town with friends.

—We're making efforts to abduct you and your sister, Sinden said jocularly to Evelyn. —Paul wants to give you girls a lift: somewhere, anywhere. The night outside is not only dismal: it's also young. I know a little place we can get a drink after hours, something that doesn't taste of dead animals. Surely nobody wants to go to bed yet?

—No matter how dog tired I am, I can't sleep, Paul volunteered unexpectedly with a drunk's solipsism, more or less talking to himself. —Soon as the old head hits the pillow, bang! Whole caboodle starts up again, the merry-go-round. Yet I slept like a top when I was a kid.

Evelyn said she didn't want a lift, though it was very kind. She'd rather get the bus.

—No monkeying around, Sinden assured her. —Evelyn, I swear. If you want to go straight home, we'll take you straight home. But there's a business proposition I'd like to discuss with your sister.

She looked at Moira anxiously. —What kind of business proposition?

—A good friend of mine is in lingerie, Sinden said. —Very exclusive and expensive. He has a salon and a small workshop in London, and I'm aware he's wanting to expand into dress design. All I'm saying is that I'd like to take a look at Moira's portfolio – not tonight of course, but some other time. If I thought her work was good, then I could introduce her to my friend. At least let me give you my card, Moira, with my telephone number.

Moira said it was an interesting idea and she would think about it; she took the card and put it in her purse; Sinden insisted again that in the meantime they should come for a spin in the Bentley. —I'm happy to take the wheel, if you're afraid Paul's had a few too many.

Evelyn was about to insist that she'd rather not, when Moira seized her by the arm and jerked her away. —Wait for us here, she said to Sinden. —We'll get our coats, then we need to pop upstairs and powder our noses.

—But I don't *want* to, Moira, Evelyn protested sotto voce, as her sister pulled her towards the bar. —I hate those men.

—Just follow me, Moira hissed, not letting go her grip. They found their coats and Evelyn's bag; when

Evelyn saw Donald watching her, solitary across the room, she was smitten with compunction. He'd enjoy those words, too: *smitten*, and *compunction*. Perhaps before she left she'd dance with him once more, even though he was hopeless. The sisters hesitated, coats over their arms, at the foot of a dark stair; they'd seen girls disappearing up here in the course of the evening, presumably in search of the toilet; impossible to tell, when those girls came down again, if they'd been successful. The men just went to pee whenever they needed, in the harbour outside. —Is there a Ladies upstairs? they asked Vincent, who looked doubtful and said not many ladies drank in the Packet as a rule.

Evelyn was hesitant. —We could wait until we got home.

—I can't wait.

Now they'd imagined relieving themselves, they were both desperate to go. It was very dark on the stairs. Evelyn discovered a light switch and tried it, but nothing came on; they felt their way hanging on to a sticky handrail. Moira found a book of matches in her handbag and struck one; when a promising door on a half-landing only led into a cupboard full with sacks of mouldy sawdust and scurrying noises, she shut it again quickly. —Mice, she decreed, and struck another match. By the matches' wavering feeble light – they were only little paper ones, the kind they give you in hotels – they climbed the boxy winding wood-panelled staircase and peered into rooms, one after another, of an extraordinary ancientness and awfulness. Some had their windows boarded up; in others they could make out, by a dim light creeping through filthy windowpanes, looming forms that might have been rolled-up drugget, broken chairs, crates full of bottles, coiled rope, heaps of white china crockery, old clothes, boots, oars, a birdcage, a painted sign lying on its side. Staves of a barrel, whose hoops had burst, fanned in a toothy grin. Each time a match went out, the dank smell of the place – tarry and rotten – settled on them like the whole foul weight of the past. —I suppose this would be Vincent's idea of heaven, said Moira disparagingly. The top floor was emptier, but still none of these rooms was any kind of bathroom or toilet; in one of them where iron bedsprings were propped against one wall and the torn old wallpaper was printed with flower baskets, Evelyn wailed that she was desperate. —Oh, I'm just going to go right here, Moira exclaimed.

Evelyn squealed. —You can't! Moira!

—I can! No one will ever know. The place stinks anyway. Hold my coat, will you, and strike another match for me? I don't want to get pee on my dress.

They were probably both drunker than they realised. Moira hoiked up her skirt and petticoat, pulled down her knickers, spread her legs, and peed against the wall with a satisfying splashing. —God, that's good, she laughed. And when she'd finished she struck the last match for Evelyn – who had more difficulty, tugging her tight slacks down.

—What if anyone comes? What about rats?

—Well, hurry up then.

Evelyn screamed while she peed, imagining the rats. When the match went out, while she struggled to pull up her clothes, Moira told her that Cass was dead.

—What?

—I heard that he died. His mother wrote to me last week, at the art college. He was ambushed, I suppose he was shot, just like the man said. It was all my fault. Which is what his mother more or less thinks too.

Evelyn stood frozen with her slacks halfway up her thighs. —Oh Moira. Oh no.

—I feel so awful. He said he'd sign up if I wouldn't go with him to Paris.

She pulled up her slacks, for decorum. —That doesn't make it your fault.

—I told him I didn't love him. That I loved someone else.

Moira sobbed just once, or at least Evelyn thought it was a sob: an ugly barking noise, roughly torn out of her, almost like exasperation. When Evelyn tried to console her, Moira pushed her away, wiping her eyes brusquely with the back of her hand. Evelyn sobbed too, in sympathy with her sister: she couldn't truly grieve for Robert Cassidy, she realised, because she'd hardly known him. His death was too improbable – he had seemed so solidly alive, with his loud laugh, the explosion of his freckles. As the girls grew used to the dark, each could make out the other's shape: the darkness anyhow seemed thinner up here at the top of the building. Glass must be broken in a window, because the wind whistled and a draught blew around their shoulders.

—So who is the someone else?

—I can't tell you. Because it isn't really anything. Not yet.

—Who, though? You have to tell!

Moira couldn't repress a voluptuous satisfaction in her voice. —The trumpet player.

Evelyn felt like a fool. Of course it was: with his forbidding frown and his high notes. She saw, in a flash of revelation, that Moira had been performing that entire evening, and dancing and flirting with Paul and all those other men, for the eyes of the trumpet player only. —And does he know? I mean, what you feel about him?

—He sort of knows. He knows, yes. Though he's still with someone else right now.

In her sister's expression – vivid even in the dimness, and so familiar from their childhood – Evelyn saw recklessness, fear, concealment, power. Moira had made such efforts to transform herself, when they moved down to Bristol, into this controlled, poised young woman. Yet some essence of the fierce bold child persisted in her, and had been diverted into new channels, sexual and personal.

—And now, Moira declared. —We have to get away from those hideous men.

—I thought you liked them!

—I hate them. I could kill them.

Light came weakly, on the landing of this upper floor, through a half-glassed metal-framed door at one end, which led onto a fire escape. Moira tried the door handle, tugging it abruptly so that the door opened inwards and boisterous wet night rushed in. —I thought so, she exclaimed in triumph, voice whipping away from her in the blast.

—No, Moy, I can't. I'm not going down there. Not in a thousand years.

—You can!

—Why don't we just go downstairs normally and insist on getting the bus home?

—Because you can never get away from that kind of man. They'll inveigle us into something or other and then it'll be too late.

Evelyn was sure she could have got away from them easily. But Moira had buttoned up her coat already, and stepped out onto the rickety, rusty platform. Evelyn screamed again: didn't the fire escape sway, away from the stuccoed side of the building? —It's fine, Moira reassured her. —Just a little bit shaky. I'll go first.

This was more or less what she'd said all those years ago, when they'd walked on the metal struts across the glasshouse roof in the park, up in the north. Which hadn't ended well: Moira had put her foot through the glass and needed twelve stitches, they'd got into serious trouble. At least this fire escape was a proper stairway, with a bannister to hold on to, and not just one of those ladders attached to a wall. Moira ran down swiftly and lightly, with a jangle of her heels on the iron, to the bottom: which was still about six foot off the ground, in an open yard at the side of the pub. Then she jumped, landing gracefully in a crouch on all fours like a cat, pale coat billowing around her in the wet.

—See! It's easy.

Evelyn stood on the narrow platform at the top, sick and dizzy and exalted, while the wind flew at her and threw rain at her. Lights on the ships in the Basin and on the wharves were reflected in the black water: beyond the harbour she could make out the great masses of the city against the night sky, its ghostly terraces climbing the hills. How could she take in that Cass was dead, while she was still alive and young? All the kingdoms of the world, and the glory of them, were in that giddy moment spread beneath her.

Evelyn made her way down the fire escape, more cautiously than Moira, then hesitated at the bottom.

—Throw me your bag, Moira said. —What's in it?

—A dress I wore so that they couldn't see me. And Mam's umbrella.

—She'll be annoyed. It's her whist drive tonight.

—Oh Moira, are you full of grief?

—Just jump, said Moira impatiently. —Trust me.

And Evelyn jumped and she was all right. She was jubilant, landing in a crunch of gravel beside her sister, though the jolt shocked all thought out of her body for a moment, down there in that filthy salty bitter underworld of dark, and her palms stung from the sharpness of the stones.

2

Old Fright

The sisters had to share a bedroom, whenever Moira was at home. Evelyn woke first and studied, sleepily, her sister's profile in the next bed; the early morning light was veiled and ethereal, filtered through silky lilac curtains at the window. Even before she properly remembered yesterday and Vincent's party, she knew that it was Sunday: the house was hushed and somnolent and sounds from outside were subdued. One of the dock cranes was unloading freight but its creaking and clanging, and the men's voices calling, seemed to come from far off, other-worldly. Moira was more severe in her sleep, and her nose was sharper. She frowned and ground her teeth, pink dribble had dried on her cheek from the blackcurrant she'd put in her cider, and her lace-trimmed pillowcase was smudged with mascara and powder. They'd been too drunk and tired last night, when they got back on the bus from the party, to cold-cream their faces. Evelyn could hear their brother Ned creeping about downstairs. He liked having the house to himself before anyone else got up. She wasn't aware of dozing off again, until Ned cracked open the door to peer in, checking to see if Moira had come home.

Everyone was glad when Moira was home. She scolded them, but her energy and determination straightened them out. Standards slipped when Evelyn and Mam and Ned were left alone together: the washing-up wasn't done, Evelyn and Mam would read for half the day in their dressing gowns if they could get away with it, Ned prowled off to make explosives in the shed. Their family life seemed to be thinning out. Sometimes all five of them still slept in the house overnight, but more often recently their father and Moira stayed away. They knew their father had a girlfriend somewhere because their mother couldn't help herself telling them so, in her tirades against him. But they couldn't discuss this fact with her or among themselves, it was too shaming and appalling. They knew that he wanted a divorce. And of course their father didn't say anything to them. That shutter came down across his expression, closing them out and finding their intrusion distasteful, beneath his dignity.

Ned lingered in the bedroom doorway. He was twelve years old, tall and thickset for his age, his features – long nose, luxuriant eyebrows, eyes alert and sceptical – too adult in his young face whose flesh was unformed and doughy. He was dressed in his crumpled grey school trousers and white shirt, although obviously he wouldn't be going to school on a Sunday. In his second year at the Cathedral School he was already in trouble, although he was clever, for mitching from lessons and stealing from the chemistry lab – their father had to talk to the headmaster to stop him being expelled. Ned looked around at the mess of clothes on the bedroom floor and spotted their mother's green umbrella, still furled although it was sodden, dropped carelessly on top of Evelyn's wool dress. —She was looking everywhere for that last night. You'll be in trouble.

—Is Dad here?

They weren't afraid of their mother, unless she enlisted their father against them.

—His shoes are on the mat. He must have come in late. Even later than you.

—I needed the umbrella. I've lost mine, I think I left it in the church room.

Ned whistled: softly, because Moira and their parents were still sleeping. —You won't half catch it.

Evelyn pulled herself up on her elbows in the bed, drunkenness from last night sloshing poisonously inside her. —Not if you don't tell. I'll put it back and she won't ever know. Don't you dare tell.

—It'll cost you.

—Or I might tell on you, what I heard about your exploding balloon on the bus. That's a lot worse than borrowing any old umbrella.

—How do you know about that?

—I just know, from somebody.

Ned looked gratified that news of his exploits had travelled. That balloon had taken a lot of preparation, soaking string for a fuse in sodium chlorate weed-killer from the garden shed, dissolving milk-bottle tops in a solution of caustic soda in a milk bottle. The first time he tried it the bottle had got very hot and cracked, leaking deadly caustic onto the garden path. He'd managed eventually to stretch a balloon over the bottleneck, inflating it with hydrogen.

—I'll bet it's Mrs Magnus. She's a busybody.

—It's not her. She's had a stroke, poor old thing. Not because of your stupid balloon, don't flatter yourself. It was months ago.

—It would be kinder to put them down, Ned said sententiously.

—We're supposed to go round and see her.

—I'm not going anywhere near her.

—You're saying that because you're scared, in case she's deformed and frightful.

When Evelyn leered and lunged at her brother

from her pillow, letting her jaw drop vacantly and crossing her eyes, Ned jumped back, then pretended he hadn't. Their conflict was mostly companionable – they bickered, but amiably. They were talking now in low, confiding voices. He told her that their parents were going out this evening, to some swanky do.

—Really? She didn't say. On a Sunday?

—Cocktail reception. On *The Flying Fox*. She didn't know until he told her yesterday.

—Mam will be pleased, if he's being nice to her.

—She is pleased.

—Keeping up appearances. Can't turn up at the reception without wifie in tow.

Ned waited in the doorway, jigging on the balls of his feet with his hands in his pockets, looking over at Moira. —She's got crud on her cheek. What did you two get up to last night?

—None of your business, Evelyn said. —Nothing.

Scowling, without opening her eyes, Moira scrubbed at her cheek with the sheet, then heaved up the blankets almost over her head, turning her back on them, hanging onto her dreams. The bedroom smelled strongly of her sweat and her perfume, signs of her body so much further advanced into womanly experience; when Evelyn had the room to herself its air seemed thin and virginal.

—God, I'm so ill, Moira groaned. —What's the matter with me?

Conspiratorial, her brother and sister exchanged glances. *Hangover*, mouthed Ned. Famously, Moira was always complaining that she was ill. As a child, up in the north, she'd stayed off school for days on end because of her asthma; her breathing would only ease if their father, whose favourite she was, sat reading to her until she fell asleep. She'd got into the habit, Evelyn thought, of managing her family like this. Nowadays the ups and downs of Moira's illnesses were a force in themselves, bending their moods to her well-being.

*   *   *

Evelyn hung her dress on its hanger and opened the umbrella to dry it off, then got dressed for Sunday school, demure in her navy skirt and the broderie anglaise white blouse which matched her New Testament, bound in white leather, her grandmother's christening present. None of them went to church these days except for her. Their mother had grown up as a Catholic, but when they moved south she left all that behind her, along with her family and their whole world. Her religion meant though that she wouldn't contemplate divorce. Ned claimed he'd come up with mathematical proof that God didn't exist, and Evelyn knew that her own religious phase, which had been fervid for a while in its intensity, was drawing to an inevitable close. It wasn't possible to pray on your knees for God to preserve your innocence, and in the same life go to parties at the Steam Packet. She only went on turning up at the Anglican church conscientiously – their father was Anglican, if he was anything – because she dreaded disappointing the vicar and the other Sunday school teachers, who believed in her performance of meekness and sweetness.

Mam was frying bacon in the kitchen; Moira was drinking tea, white-faced, wrapped in a shawl in an armchair in the dining room. Their dad was kneeling, almost sacerdotal, at the dining-room hearth, making a fire, the sight of his upturned heels incongruous because he was such a tall man, used to filling space with his upright authority. He held a sheet of newspaper across the fireplace to make it blaze, which their mother had expressly warned them never to do – a coal miner's daughter, she was full of horror stories which fascinated Ned, where the newspaper flying up the chimney set fire to the soot, or detonators from the mine were left behind accidentally in the coal. As soon as the fire was burning, Dad stood up and brushed off the knees of his trousers, pleased with his own competence, slicking back the black hair from his temples, handsome with his dog-eyes and heavy cheeks. His children looked at him surreptitiously to gauge his mood; affable and even approachable, Evelyn thought. He would be satisfied because he'd arranged things smoothly for this evening. He liked to command whatever scene he was in; no doubt he was genuinely a good leader of men, admired and respected by his subordinates. Moira cherished a memory of walking with him once through the streets in the north, in his RNVR uniform, when he was on leave from the war. Rough men who squatted on their haunches to smoke, on the pavement outside the doors in Asylum Square, had leapt to their feet to salute him.

Evelyn slipped into her place beside Ned at the table. With weighty joviality, Dad asked how their party had gone. Evelyn was spreading margarine studiously on her bread – she'd instructed Moira to tell them that the party was in the Vic Rooms. Even when Evelyn was dressed for church, she was in danger of touching off some irritation in her father if she said anything, because he liked people to be natural, and found his younger daughter histrionic. As for Ned, he'd perfected some way of making himself more or less invisible; father and son had scarcely spoken since that episode at school. Moira yawned in her armchair. —It was all right. A bit dull. The same old crowd. I'm sure I've caught some germ. There's a nasty fluey thing going around.

—Your sister behaved herself?

—I kept an eye on her. Made sure that she only

drank orange squash. We came home together on the bus. An awful drunk Dutch sailor kept falling asleep with his head on my shoulder. I gave up pushing him off in the end, just let him sleep.

—The band was decent, wasn't it? Evelyn said. —Especially the trumpet player.

—Was it decent? Moira glanced sinisterly at Evelyn. —I didn't really notice.

Holding the plate in a tea towel, Mam brought in Dad's bacon and eggs and fried bread. —Mind the plate now. It's piping hot.

—Thank you, Rose.

—How is it?

He nodded with his mouth full. —Is this that bacon I got for you?

Standing over him, watching him tuck in to his breakfast, their mother was eager for his approval; she was even pretty, with colour in her cheeks, although Moira would be in despair over her slopping around in slippers, in a shapeless housecoat with curlers in her hair. Rose's skin was only faintly creased, soft and matte like a peach; her eyes and hair were dark brown, she was eager and warm. Yet her abject dependency, and her despair over their father, were too flamboyant and extreme; she carried this morning's happiness like a brimming dish that at some point would crash down, spilling everywhere. At least they were talking to each other. For days on end they would only communicate through their children, even if they were in the same room. *Tell your father his dinner is in the oven. Tell your mother I'll be back late.* They still had in common those ripe, warm accents which marked them apart from everyone around them, stamped them with the different character of the north-east. Moira and Evelyn and Ned had needed to lose their accents as soon as they could, when they started school in the south. Their new friends and their enemies had found their voices comical, no one could understand them: *book* instead of *buk*, and *mi* instead of *my*, and *canny*, and *clamming*.

Dad was pleased with the bacon. He was always bringing in some bargain or other from the docks, although he didn't tolerate any fiddling or smuggling. They'd had bananas, pineapples, badminton rackets, silks for Moira to make into dresses, quilts stitched by American ladies years ago for the war effort, which had been left to rot in a warehouse. Standing up now, pushing back his chair, wiping his mouth with the linen napkin set out for him, he said that he had to go into the office.

—Put a plate of dinner up for me, I'll eat it when I get in. I'll be back in plenty of time to take you to the *Fox*.

They saw how Rose wavered then, and almost teetered into the usual querulousness. *I suppose you're going to see her.* But she pulled herself back from that edge, reprieving them all and giving him the benefit of the doubt, perhaps because it made life easier, perhaps because she was even tired of herself sometimes, harping on the inevitable subject. She helped Dad solicitously into his greatcoat, found his muffler and gloves, closed the side door behind him. The atmosphere always lightened when their father went out, and yet they hung on – or at least his wife and daughters did – to the promise of his return. A man validated the reality of a family and gave it gravitas. If Moira ever had a husband, she said – and she had no plans, so they needn't get excited – she'd order her married life quite differently. She'd work a lot harder on her appearance than Mam did, to begin with. And the place was a mess, it wasn't exactly enticing for Dad to come home to.

Moira announced that she couldn't touch breakfast, she was too poorly, then sat at the table and picked at her plate until she'd finished it. Mam knitted in her chair, one long needle tucked under her arm, the other one darting and weaving into the stitches; at the end of the row she held up the sleeve against Ned's outstretched arm for measuring, then ran the free needle through her hair to grease it, which Moira said was disgusting.

— You girls ought to go and visit Mrs Magnus.

Ned crossed his eyes and did the gibbering thing silently, behind his mother's back.

—She's lonely and sick, poor old thing. And she was good to you two, when we first came down.

When their family first moved to Avonmouth, they'd been housed in an old farm on the estuary while the Authority sorted out a home for them; arriving back from school on the bus, the girls had to wait on the docks with this woman, who was the widow of a Norwegian ship's captain and ran the Mission to Seamen, until their father could give them a lift out to the farm. Mrs Magnus had made a fuss of them, given them tea and homemade scones and shortbread. Because that farm was a romantic but feral place, with its oil lamps and foxes and outside toilet, the girls had looked forward to those hours of respite at the Mission, doing their homework on Mrs Magnus's table spread with oilcloth, to the sound of the puttering gas fire, in her tidy parlour with its scrubbed linoleum and rag rugs. In the hallway the frightening strutting or shambling sailors had come and gone more or less peaceably, signing in at the front desk, pushing over the chit they were given on board ship. Mrs Magnus seemed able to say a few words to all of them, in their different languages.

Pulling on her coat for church and returning her mother's umbrella inconspicuously to the hallstand, Evelyn promised to call in and see Mrs Magnus in the afternoon. Moira said she'd see how she felt later, if she was well enough. —And what are you going to wear to the reception this evening? Evelyn and I will help you to get ready. I want to do your face. You should put on the nice blue I made you, with the velvet bodice.

Rose frowned and counted stitches, said she didn't care what she wore. Why should they bother with her, when she was just an old fright?

—We want you to be *soignée*, Mam.

—*Soignée* indeed, she said. —My foot. *Tray bien. San Fairy Ann.*

—I hate that Froggy language, Ned protested. —What's even the point of us learning it? What's wrong with good old English?

-*Ça ne fait rien*, Evelyn supplied in her best accent. —Which means: it doesn't matter. Doesn't matter in the least, not a fig, not one bit.

Rose wanted to know about their party. She took a great interest in all her daughters' friends, and loved Vincent, who charmed her – he was her image of a bohemian artist. Mam seemed to think that he was Moira's boyfriend, and Moira didn't disabuse her. There was no mention of Robert Cassidy, but why would there be? Their parents had never known about Moira's engagement, if it really was ever an engagement. The horrible fact of Cass's death, whenever it flared in Evelyn's thoughts, only seemed a part of the excesses of last night. His death couldn't be real, not mixed up here in all the ordinary squalor of their breakfast table, and the comforting soft clacking and flickering of Mam's knitting.

*   *   *

One evening a year or so ago, when Evelyn was alone in the house in Avonmouth – Dad was out, Moira was in town, Mam must have been at one of her whist drives, Ned was with his friend David who lived round the corner, and had the same scientific mindset – a man had rung the doorbell. Evelyn padded down the hallway to answer it in her stockinged feet, still thinking about the Peninsula War which she was studying for homework. She could see the man's shape through the glass of the porch door, he was carrying something.

—Is your dad at home?

—He's not here, sorry.

All alone in the house, Evelyn should have had Winnie the bulldog to protect her. But Winnie had escaped at some point from the back garden as usual, tunnelling furiously under the fence, and no one could be bothered to look for her. It was that dog's aim in life to dig her way out from their home, even if after a few hours she would come trotting in again docilely at the front door. They said she was trying to find her way back to Tyneside. Evelyn was sure of what the man was carrying even before she had time to look properly, except that for a moment she thought Winnie was still alive, and the man had brought her back safely. He was upset and sorry and also faintly aggrieved, afraid he'd get the blame for what had happened.

—I didn't have a chance to stop, it just ran right out in front of me.

—She does that, dashes out. She's so silly. She thinks she's playing games with the cars or something.

—Neighbour said it was yours. Tell your dad I'm sorry.

The dog was still warm when he handed her over, and seemed surprisingly heavier than when she was alive. Evelyn was appalled, and had no idea what she should do with her, so carried her through the house and put her down on the scullery table, whose white enamel top was somehow surgical and appropriate; then she thought she could go back to her books and nothing would have changed. She hadn't even been particularly fond of Winnie, it was Ned who would be heartbroken. But the words of her history book wouldn't cohere on the page in front of her eyes, and seemed to be full of horror – you couldn't just put a dead body down on a table as though it was so much meat. She got up again and went to stand beside Winnie, and tried to remember things about her, to make herself sad: how she used to get on the bus from time to time, and the conductors all knew to drop her off at the docks gate, or how she'd snaffled up the overripe Williams pears that fell out of the tree, when they lived out at the farm, until she made herself sick.

It was all right as long as Evelyn could see Winnie's body. But as soon as she moved away she suffered from a hallucination of the dog's warm weight in her arms, her savoury stuffy smell, the greasy nap of her short coat, the muscle and sinew packed so purposefully tightly, though now to no avail, inside her skin. And absurdly and embarrassingly – because Winnie after all was only a dog – when Evelyn remembered Robert Cassidy the same sensations came back to her, as if something ugly and dreadful and unwanted had been dropped into her arms, which wasn't strictly speaking anything to do with her.

* * *

The rituals of the church were supposed to console her for all this, and to some extent on that Sunday after the party they worked. Although their particular church was squat and unbeautiful – built in red brick when the Avonmouth docks were expanding in the thirties, then damaged in the war, and looking more like a customs office than any soaring aspiration to other worlds – at least it was a place where death was spoken of. Indeed it was spoken of a great deal, in the old hymns. *Ride on! ride on in majesty! / In lowly pomp ride on to die.* Or, *Thou, most kind and gentle death, / Waiting to hush our latest breath, / O praise him, alleluia!* It perplexed Evelyn that there was such a mismatch between the lurid passionate words of the hymns and the tame chit-chat of the congregation at the end of services, when any mention of death – or for that matter lowly pomp, or even riding – would have seemed jarring and excessive. Their conversation was all about deploring the quality of mince on sale at the butcher's shop, or raising money for the vicar's pet project. He had his heart set on installing a central heating system to replace the coal furnace, which leaked noxious fumes in the winter and put the congregation to sleep, or gave them headaches.

For as long as Evelyn went through the familiar motions – sitting down and standing up and singing heartily with the rest of them, kneeling and closing her eyes to pray, resting her forehead against her clasped hands, gloves scented with eau de cologne – then the space still mostly felt enchanted and sacred, she was buoyed up and soothed. From time to time, however, she was washed through with the evil aftermath of her gin and orange, and then when she remembered herself at the party in her figure-hugging black outfit, or Paul with his corrupted angel beauty, she knew that the light of this religion was too pale and shallow, and couldn't encompass the whole reality of what she wanted. She was teaching her Sunday school class that week, as it happened, about St Paul, and each time she spoke his name couldn't help herself picturing that other Paul, drunken and dissolute. Presumably dissolute: this hadn't been put to the test.

The children drew maps of the saint's voyages in their exercise books, shading in the sea with blue, marking with red dots those places where he'd visited the early Christian communities: Corinth and Antioch, Ephesus and Philippi. The kind of children whose parents sent them to Sunday school were mostly compliant, and bent their blond and brown heads quietly over their books; the sound of their pencil crayons scribbling was soporific. Classes took place in the church room, a low-ceilinged extension to the original building, with its own paraffin heater; gouts of wet sleet came thudding against the windows. Luckily Evelyn had found her umbrella, on top of the upright piano where she'd left it. She was quite a favourite with the Sunday school children, and the vicar's wife had said she had a vocation as a teacher. Her performance today, describing the saint's conversion on the road to Damascus, had been striking. — I don't think that St Paul was an easy man. I should think he was quite difficult to live with. Perhaps greatness is always like that. What do you think? If you have a great vision of the truth of things, it's hard to come down to the level of everyday life. Do you think that great men – or even great women – are always gentle and kind? We might wonder if even Jesus himself was always kind. He shouted at his disciples sometimes, reproaching them.

The boys and girls gazed at her blankly, expectantly, but possibly with inklings that what she said might be dangerous or unorthodox. When Moira appeared in the church room, toward the end of the class, she must have looked to the startled children like a vision of worldly temptation, handsome and unsmiling in her high heels and silk scarf and camel coat, with her face made up, wafting scent, shaking out her own umbrella fiercely. She had told Mam, she said when the children had gone, that she and Evelyn would visit Mrs Magnus together, on their way home for dinner. Evelyn, under the influence of her piety, readied herself to be compassionate towards the poor old lady. Moira's face was set and grim. —Come on then, let's get this over with.

*   *   *

The ground floor at the Mission to Seamen was given over to a concert hall and dance floor, and there was a skittle alley in the basement, used as an air-raid shelter in the war. These facilities didn't look as if they'd been opened up recently. The place had lost the homely gloss it had when the sisters used to come there after school. Rugs in the hallway were filthy with wet dirt and despite the weather the door stood open to the street. The parlour where the girls had once done their homework was being used for storage; they waited in there among stacks of chairs and cardboard boxes full of religious leaflets. A scurrying and bothered young woman came from the kitchen, to show them where Mrs Magnus was being looked after, in one of the rooms on the top floor; she led them up an echoing flight of steps of polished concrete, with an iron handrail. The Mission was actually a gracious building, bigger and more ambitious than the church, put up before the Depression, austerely municipal yet flooded with light from the tall windows. Mrs Magnus had no family, the woman said, there was nowhere else for her to go. The nurse came in twice a day, to help look after her, and anyhow she wasn't absolutely incapacitated. She could get herself out of bed and into her chair, or onto the commode. She could still feed herself, if the meals were cut up for her.

When Moira and Evelyn were shown into the room, they hardly recognised the woman they'd once known. When they last saw Mrs Magnus she was capable and powerful and kind, baking scones and tea loaves and shortbread biscuits, keeping the Mission scrubbed and clean. She'd looked after all those sailors who were far away from home, and overseen social activities for them: there were dances on Saturdays to which the sisters weren't allowed to come, because they were unsuitable. Bustling and solicitous in her capacious checked apron, Mrs Magnus in those days had been padded out with flesh; her chestnut hair, only flecked with grey, was pinned tidily in a fat bun. Now her hair was white and hung loose on her shoulders, her face seemed longer and hollowed out, her teeth were pushed forward in a new leering prominence in her sunken mouth. Shrunken, child-size, she sat in an armchair beside her narrow bed, dressing gown pulled on crookedly over a creased grubby nightdress. When the sisters were shown in she leaned forward eagerly, but that might have only been because she'd been sitting alone for hours, since the nurse last came. They couldn't tell whether she recognised them or not. The room smelled unpleasant, and its window looked out onto the brick wall of a warehouse.

No one had bothered to mention that Mrs Magnus couldn't speak. She stared keenly at her visitors, as if she had something urgent to communicate, she made noises and gestured, and the girls tried to understand her. Did she want water? Was she warm enough? Wasn't this weather dreadful? The woman from the kitchen, they assured her, had promised to bring up tea. They had no idea how much the old lady understood of what they said, or whether she even knew who they were. They babbled on about their own news, which could only sound cruelly gloating. Or they dredged up every reminiscence they could, about the old days when she'd been strong and able and looked after them: that might have been a cruelty too. Impatiently, emphatically, Mrs Magnus made her garbled noise again. Of course they could guess the fundamentals of what she wanted to communicate. They could see what news she brought: it was in front of their eyes. Evelyn wondered whether all of her visitors, if she had any other visitors – surely some of those sailors came up to see her? – were as cowardly as they were, avoiding naming what was obvious. Maybe no words were adequate, to express what had befallen Mrs Magnus.

When they couldn't understand her, she seemed to be angry with them – and why shouldn't she be? Evelyn meanwhile was bargaining with herself, asking herself how much she would be able to bear. If you could see one tree outside your window, would that be enough to live for? If you could see the sky at least: a nun or an anchorite could make a whole spiritual life out of a patch of sky, or less. Tea was brought up from the kitchen, and that passed some time: Mrs Magnus had to have hers in a cup with a spout, and it dribbled on her chin. The girls escaped after sitting with her for half an hour – she'd had enough of them anyway, waving her hand in a dismissal which was contemptuous of their failure to understand her, or change anything for her. They hurried downstairs and out into the street, hardly caring about the sleety rain blowing in their faces. —I will never, ever, allow myself to be like that, Moira said as they strode along – emphatically, as if she were furious about something.

Evelyn demurred, reasonably enough. —But you might not be able to help it. Poor Mrs Magnus, she couldn't help having a stroke. She didn't want to have one.

—I tell you I won't. I won't let it happen to me.

—But what would you do? I mean, if you were her, and it just caught you unawares?

—I'd never be her. I'd do something. I'd find some way to finish myself off.

Evelyn wanted to push back against what her sister was saying, her wild presumption. Weren't we all helpless to defend ourselves, against whatever depredations and losses and suffering were in store for us? But Moira's will really was something extraordinary. Perhaps in the future, if ever she got seriously ill, or even if she just grew old, then she would manage somehow, through her sheer force of character, to sustain her elegance and her control. Perhaps she would insist, all the way to the end, on keeping up with the world and being competent in it. She would refuse to become pathetic or ridiculous, she would hang on to her elderly beauty and know how to tend to it, which creams to use on her face, how to make up her eyes to hide the shadows and the sagging. She would still be charming and funny and attract new friends. Even if that did happen, though, it could never be known finally whether it had anything to do with Moira's will; it might only be the working out of chance.

And perhaps because Evelyn was more yielding and self-doubting and hesitant, or perhaps just by chance, when she grew old she might give in sooner than her big sister, relinquishing her strength and her self and becoming direly forgetful and dotty in her old age, her extreme old age, losing names and eating at strange times of day and setting fire to things on the stove – though she wouldn't ever be as bad as Mrs Magnus, never that desperate or unhappy. And Moira might chivvy Evelyn and despair of her, ashamed of the dirty old jumper and dresses she wore, exhorting her to hold on to her self and her dignity for just a little bit longer, just long enough. Perhaps all this would come about eventually for the two sisters, at the end of the long decades that lay ahead, and the long stories of their marriages and their children, and all the unfolding adventures of their living.

* * *

At home the windows dripped with steam from Rose's cooking. Sunday dinner – roast lamb, mint sauce, roast potatoes, carrots, cabbage, mashed parsnip, steamed pudding and custard – was the grand climax to all the cooking and eating of the week. A white damask cloth was laid over a blanket, to protect the mahogany table from the hot dishes; silver knives and forks were taken out from their canteen lined in white satin, which had been a wedding present; they all had their own linen napkins, kept over from week to week to save on washing. The kitchen meanwhile was in disarray and Rose, still in her curlers tied in a scarf, sweated and cursed: *Hell's bells and blinking panthers.* The sink was full of peelings, pan lids rattled and bubbled on the stove, boiling fat slopped onto the floor when the potatoes were basted, the gravy had to be made at the last minute in the meat tin, with flour and vegetable water and gravy browning from a crusted, ancient bottle. When the meal was on the table they ate heartily; Rose was a good cook. The pudding was a perfect golden dome studded with currants, served with Bird's custard, although Moira lamented that it was bad for her figure. A savoury fatty fragrance of dinner, hanging everywhere in the house for hours afterwards, was part of the atmosphere of Sunday afternoons.

Mam might have taken her curlers out if Dad had come home; it was eccentric to sit down in curlers at a table laid with damask and silver. But then Rose was eccentric, she was wayward and rash: these were her husband's complaints precisely. The girls had to keep their mother's spirits up, transport her safely across the fact of his absence; they chattered and joked and teased her, set out his meal on a plate for warming up later. Then when they'd finished eating, Moira took command. She tied on her mother's apron and sat Rose down in an armchair with the *Sunday Express* crossword and a glass of sherry; rolling up her sleeves, she set about restoring order. Moira had a gift, astute and decisive as any military tactician, for cleaning and tidying. As usual she complained that Evelyn was too dreamy and too slow. Ned set off a smoke bomb in the front room, made from a ping-pong ball and silver foil; he was sent upstairs in disgrace and they had to open the windows, wasting all the warmth built up inside. Rose was saying that on second thoughts she didn't want to go out to the reception.

All this chaos of life at home was smothering and intolerable sometimes, and the sisters couldn't wait to get away into lives of their own. This afternoon, though, they were filled with exuberant energy and laughter, in spite of the dinner weighing like lead in their stomachs. At the end of an hour they were triumphant: everything was put away, the kitchen was wiped around everywhere, the floor was swept, wet tea towels hung across the stove to dry. While Evelyn made a pot of tea, Moira dabbed at the hem of her coat with alcohol, where it was muddy from the night

70

before. When Rose woke up from dozing she asked for news of poor old Mrs Magnus, and Evelyn said it was such a shame she was left alone all day; she would try to call in from time to time. Moira said, —What's the point? She didn't even want us. Ned came sidling downstairs, asking for tea.

*   *   *

Their mother put on the blue dress Moira had made her, with an A-line brocade skirt and velvet bodice, cut with a draped neck and three-quarter sleeves. Inevitably the strap on her petticoat was broken, Moira had to lend her a safety pin. They sat her down at the walnut-veneer dressing table in her bedroom. —Old fright, she said, gazing mercilessly at her reflection, but coquetting her head on her neck none-theless, out of habit. She wasn't really old, she was forty-three, but that seemed old enough to her daughters, their youthful beauty crowded into the reflection in the mirror beside hers, affecting not to look at themselves, only stealing side glances. Then Moira took her mother's face between her hands and turned it toward her, bringing her own face close so that they mirrored each other, each unconsciously mimicking the other's expression. Catching the tip of her tongue between her teeth in concentration, Moira smoothed Basic Dew onto her mother's worn cheeks, then powdered them and gave them a faint touch of colour, pencilling in the arch of her eyebrows and painting her eyes with eyeliner and mascara.

—Not too much, Rose anxiously said.

—Trust me. It won't be too much.

Working tenderly around her wedding ring, Evelyn rubbed lotion into those hands which still smelled of cooking, then painted her mother's nails absorbedly with Cherry Ripe. They all three had the same small hands and feet, bony and fine, but the skin on Rose's hands was growing loose. They searched in the dressing-table drawer for her green enamelled necklace and matching earrings; her jewellery case was jumbled in with her girdles and stockings and brassieres and spectacles and used ration books, nightdresses and knitted bedjackets, old letters and postcards and handkerchiefs and hairpins and boxes of pills. Somewhere in there too, wrapped in tissue paper, was the long plait she'd cut off by herself with scissors when she was sixteen, because she wanted a marcel wave, in defiance of her parents.

The sweet stale smell of that drawer, face powder and wool and witch hazel, still had its mystique and suggestion of glamour for Rose's daughters. When they were children they weren't supposed to go rummaging in their mother's things, and the dressing table had seemed a temple then, its back to the window, its bottle of Je Reviens by Worth and its cut-glass ring tray and jar of cold cream, the crocheted lace doilies set under the glass top, the heavy hinged mirror sending their reflections jouncing vertiginously to the ceiling if they swung it, turning the room topsy-turvy. Doing Rose's lipstick now, Moira blotted her own lips together in demonstration, then stood behind her, judging her critically in the mirror, taking out her curlers and combing the fine dark chestnut hair into waves, spraying to hold them in place. Their father's girlfriend was supposed to be much younger and good-looking, but in that moment they were all three hopeful, fastening on the green necklace and the earrings, hearing him arrive home through the side door.

3

San Fairy Ann

Sinden telephoned on Wednesday evening, at supper time. Handing the receiver over to Moira her father was guardedly respectful, because Sinden with his assured accent sounded like a man and not a boy. The others went on eating their shepherd's pie while listening to Moira speaking levelly and coolly out in the hall. —Oh yes, hello. I see.

It wasn't the trumpet player, Evelyn thought. She knew without asking that Moira had been waiting, more impatiently with every day that passed, for a telephone call from the trumpet player. If it was him on the telephone, she wouldn't be able to keep the satisfaction out of her voice. —Yes, all right, Moira said, non-committal. —I know where that is, yes.

She didn't give any sign of being either perturbed or pleased, sitting down again at the table. —Just a friend, she said, when her mother asked her. —His sister's a friend of mine, they live in Sneyd Park. They were at Vincent's party on Saturday. They've asked us to go round this evening to play mah-jong. They'll pick us up in their car.

—Sneyd Park, that's nice.

Evelyn knew better than to query the existence of these new friends. —I'm not going anywhere, she said, —I've got work to do.

She was wearing her old skirt and slippers, her hair was a mess, and she had to prepare a translation from *Andromaque*. —Anyhow, I don't know how to play mah-jong.

—That doesn't matter, Moira said lightly, but staring pointedly at her sister. —It's only a bit of fun. They want you to come.

—I don't want to go, though.

—Don't spoil your sister's evening, their father said to Evelyn.

He probably liked the idea of them visiting in Sneyd Park. On a different occasion, their mother might have taken Evelyn's side: since Sunday, however, a fragile truce had held between their parents, and Rose for the moment was meekly devoted and obedient. The reception on *The Flying Fox* had been a success, apparently. The two of them had performed their old double act where he clowned around and pretended to play the piano, she pretended to sing: it had gone down well. When they'd finished their pudding, Moira chivvied her sister upstairs. —But I don't want to go out, Evelyn protested furiously on the landing, resisting where Moira was pushing and prodding her into the bedroom from behind, making a tease out of it.

—We'll have you all smartened up and looking lovely.

—I don't want to look lovely: not tonight. Who are these people anyway?

—That was Sinden on the telephone.

—Who?

—Those men we met at the party: remember? He's going to bring the Bentley round, to take us to Paul's house. It sounds like a laugh: we'll see how the other half lives. Apparently their house has ten bedrooms, and there are servants. Imagine a butler taking our coats at the door.

—But I hate those men. You said you hated them!

Moira agreed, she did hate them. On the other hand she was dying of boredom here, and she wanted to show Sinden her portfolio. She must be punishing the trumpet player, Evelyn guessed. Or proving to herself that she was brittle and shallow and didn't care, she could have a good time without him. —So had you given them our telephone number?

Moira said that she hadn't, she supposed they'd

got it from Vincent or someone, but Evelyn could always tell when her sister was lying.

*　*　*

It was Paul who arrived to pick them up in the car. He even got out from the driver's seat and shook hands with their father, who came to the front gate in the rain to take a look at him, and was clearly impressed with the nice-looking young man and his good manners, as well as with the Bentley. Good job he hadn't seen Paul when he was dead drunk on Saturday, Evelyn darkly thought. Luckily for the girls their father wasn't obsequious, he didn't embarrass them, he was bluff and stern and off-handed in the same way with everyone. It was obvious as soon as they set off in the car, fat tyres hissing on the wet road, that Paul couldn't remember their names, or which of them was which. —Come on, remind me, he joked to Moira in the front passenger seat.

She laughed and was disconcerted, looking away from him out of the car window at the familiar streets as they swung past. —I'm not telling you. Tweedle-dum and Tweedledee. Nora and Dora.

—It's not fair. You both look so alike. Are you twins?

Moira wouldn't like that, Evelyn thought. She was watching unseen from the back of the car, where she slumped in a corner, sulking. Nothing was right for her that evening: she longed to be at home with her French books at the kitchen table. She was sure that she looked overdressed, in the green skirt and black taffeta jacket which Moira had rather perfunctorily picked out for her; even Moira had despaired of her hair, which needed washing. And the car's motion was so smooth that Evelyn was bound to feel sick, slipping around on the leather upholstery each time they turned a corner – she wound the window down a little way. Light from the passing street lamps slid down the side of Paul's face over and over like a succession of masks, uncovering in the dusk the wide fair brow, shallowly set eye, trick of shadow on the cheek. His beauty seemed a thing apart from himself, as if he were sealed inside it, inaccessible and therefore desirable; even his authority with the gearstick and the steering wheel might undo you. He was dressed more informally than on Saturday, in a black turtleneck sweater, and his performance of charm toward them was perfunctory, indifferent – he wasn't really flirting. Evelyn was sure that it hadn't been Paul's idea in the first place, inviting them over.

They drove along the Portway, and then across the Downs into an area of the city she didn't know, where big houses were set secretively apart behind their high walls and gardens, and the street lamps illuminated only well-kempt emptiness, a few furtive cats.

Turning into a private road, and then through iron gates propped open, they climbed with a crunch of gravel under gloomy conifers; garden odours of wet earth and rotting leaves were pungent inside the car. The pale facade of a house loomed at the top of the drive, its many windows mostly dark; they drew up with a flourish before a curved, pillared porch. Paul apologised for its grandeur as they got out. —It's an awful stuffy old place.

—Is it yours? Are your parents home?

—No parents anywhere for miles, thank God. Pa long deceased. Our mama may be somewhere in the West Indies, we think – but anyhow she doesn't live here, we don't allow it. Place belongs to me and my brother Tommy, along with the girls – our sister and our cousin Viola. We'll probably get rid of it at some point, but so long as Tommy's under the weather it's convenient. Our aunt left it to us, and our uncle was lord mayor, so it's all very stiff and dreadful inside. We camp in it like kids. Just playing at being grown up, you know.

A grand staircase wound up into darkness from the dim chilly entrance hall, whose chandelier was electric, but unlit; a forbidding case clock ticked loudly and reproachfully. They left their coats and Moira's portfolio on a chair, there was no butler to take them: the staff went home at night, Paul said. Then he delivered them, with an air of discharging a duty, into the ground-floor drawing room, where a small knot of people, three men and two young women, one of the men in uniform and the women in evening dresses, were gathered around a log fire, meagre in a baronial stone hearth, talking desultorily and intimately. The long room was frigid and formal in the style of fifty years earlier. Crimson drapes with tasselled gold cords hung undrawn at the windows, framing the glass panes black with night; between the windows were Jacobean-fantasy carved oak chairs, straight backs to the wall. Three more unlit electric chandeliers hung suspended in murky darkness. This room had been imagined for quite different forms of sociability; the present company had turned their backs on it, pulling up a sofa and an armchair angled around the fire, huddling in the pink light from a couple of table lamps.

—So here are the girls, Paul announced. —I asked if they were twins. Don't you think they're alike?

The others looked up without much interest. —Not bad, said someone who must be Paul's brother Tommy because he looked ill, propped against pillows at one end of the sofa, eyes swimming in the shadows from the lamps, long neck too spindly for his shirt collar. A thin dark girl, vivid and scowling, crouched on a footstool at his feet beside the fire, arms wrapped around her knees, sharp chin resting on her clasped hands, her satiny sleeveless dress liqueur-yellow. She asked if the sisters were going to sing for their supper. Standing quite still and smiling, Moira managed to appear amused and unperturbed, outside the circle of their hostility. —It's not advisable. You've never heard us sing.

—The little witch is our sister Doll, Paul said. —And this is Podge, who's really Viola – although she won't answer if you call her that, she hates it.

—But Viola's such a dainty name! Moira exclaimed, meaning to be unkind because Podge was big-boned and clumsy and fair, with a deep bosom, her purple gown matronly.

—There's nothing to eat, you know, Podge said gruffly. —In case you did want supper.

—Oh no, we've eaten, thank you.

The little witch cackled. Moira and Evelyn were aware of hidden codes of class, embedded in the detail of dress and voice and language, which they transgressed at every moment. Was it vulgar to say that you'd eaten? Or to thank anyone, perhaps? This awareness of unavoidable pitfalls made them more daring: they had nothing to lose.

—So Paulie, Doll asked, —whatever are you going to do with these girls? Now you've gone to all this trouble to get hold of them.

Paul said he had no idea, it was Sinden who'd insisted he fetch them. The man in uniform, who sounded American – he was broad and tall and genial – suggested selling them into the white slave trade. Evelyn found herself protesting crossly that she hadn't even wanted to come, she wasn't in the mood and had a translation to do, but Moira had bullied her into it. —And I can't even play mah-jong.

—Whoever said anything about mah-jong?

—I said it, Moira explained, still smiling graciously. —So that our parents would think we were going somewhere respectable.

Doll was wide-eyed. —We're frightfully respectable here.

—We needed an injection of new blood, Sinden insisted. —To liven us up because we're all so blue.

—Are we a blood sacrifice? said Moira brightly. —Is this a horror film?

—I'm not blue, drawled Tommy, gaunt against his pillow. —Who says I'm blue?

Bustling forward from the drinks tray, proprietorial and ugly with his bulging eyes and pouchy flesh, Sinden was almost the sisters' ally in that unfriendly room, because he was familiar, and because for whatever reason he was eager, conciliatory. —But aren't these new girls fresh and lovely? Paul danced with Moira all night long on Saturday, it was the romance of the century.

—You shouldn't tease them, Paulie, Doll said.

—Moira's an artist: a dress designer! Sinden persisted. —While Evelyn knows French poetry.

The American said suggestively that he knew some French too.

—The filthy Yankee soldier is Hal, and on the sofa that's Tommy, the hypochondriac we warned you about. Such a fraud, he's fit as a fiddle. Hal's supposed to be making us cocktails. What else are the Yankees good for?

Their gathering seemed to revolve around the American, as an honoured guest who must also be teased and derided as part of homage: subtly the others vied for his attention and showed off to him, while he stood blinking and bulky, impressive, pelt of his white-blond hair clipped short, thick flesh folded on his bull neck. Leaning against the stone mantelpiece carved with a coat of arms as if this were only his due, he smoked and smiled hazily at some private joke. Sinden wasn't quite like a guest, he made himself too much at home and was too useful – when the others glanced at him they hardly seemed to see him. In the end he made the cocktails, because Hal wouldn't stir from the mantelpiece; Paul dragged a second sofa over to the fire for the sisters to sit on. Evelyn was brittle with indignation. Passionately she didn't want to be here in this room where, in between snatches of the barbed dull conversation, she could hear rain gusting and squalling against the window; it even blew down the chimney once or twice, and spat in the fire. She longed to walk out into the night and breathe it, have those braying hostile voices whipped away in a wild wind. But Moira smiled inscrutably as if she were actually enjoying herself, and the American in his lazy way began to flirt with her, so that Doll sat more upright and vigilant on her footstool.

The drinks Sinden made were very strong. Evelyn had never had martinis before: at least she liked the little olive on the stick. As the alcohol took effect they all drew closer in their enmity around the hearth, mustered against the shrouding darkness in the room behind. Moira told Hal that she liked jazz, and he offered to take her round the dives in Harlem if ever she came to New York, where she could hear some real Cotton Club music. Evelyn said that she'd love to visit Harlem, she'd heard it was an amazing place, and Hal laughed: a nice girl there would need someone to look after her, he said. — You'll have to watch out though, Tommy warned, — if it's Hal looking after you. He's got his own way of taking care of girls.

Gaunt against his pillow, the sick man was smoking and downing martinis along with the rest of them. The drink brought out a salaciousness and savagery in him, as if he exerted his strong will in talk, to compensate for his physical weakness. He complained that his brother looked like a sissy in his sweater, then lashed out at Sinden for fussing with the drinks like an old woman or a waiter. All the doctors these days were quacks growing fat on his taxes, he said, and he didn't believe in them – they didn't care whether you lived or died. He might write a book about it, while he was on the mend like this, having to hang around with time on his hands. Podge commented encouragingly that she was sure he could write, he was awfully clever.

—Fat lot of good it does me, Podge. Nobody these days wants the clever men.

Tommy put on a show of ferocious opinions: behind them, Evelyn intuited, he was seized with panic, connected to his sickness. And she didn't believe that he was clever, nor any of them – not as clever as she was. Weren't all of them wrong, with their class defensiveness and their reactionary politics, their prejudices and their wealth? They were all on the wrong side of history. Yet her confidence stumbled in this company tonight, and on their home terrain. She was full of doubt; their certainties had power here. She asked if Tommy was going to write a novel.

—God, no. Novels are a waste of time, they're for women and children. More like some sort of satire, showing up what a mess we're in, and about some of the dolts and asses they've put in charge.

—Tommy can have a great career in politics, Sinden said. —Just as soon as he's up and about again. He's only stepped back for a bit, because everything's going to the dogs.

Topping up his own glass from the gin bottle, Paul deferred to Tommy with anxious distaste, as if he dreaded his brother's suffering. —He was head boy at school, you know. Everything expected of him. Won an exhibition to Cambridge but never took it up.

—Other things to do, Tommy said crisply, with satisfaction. —There was a war to fight.

—Wish I hadn't been too young for that, Paul said.

Moira fetched her portfolio to show to Sinden, they spread her drawings out across the rug and, kneeling to peer at them, he took a great interest, said he was keen to show them to his friend who might have funding to set her up as a designer. Moira only laughed at him, said she wasn't sure yet what she wanted to do when she'd finished at art school. But she had a talent, a real talent, Sinden insisted. Didn't Doll think so? Doll lived for months at a time with her godmother in Paris, he explained to Moira, absorbing the culture and going to the fashion shows. —Sleeping with all the French men, Tommy said.

—Not all of them, darling. Some have ghastly moustaches.

Uncoiling languidly from her footstool, Doll stood

up to look at the drawings. Her silky dress, revealed at full length, really was good, cut so simply that it was almost careless, hanging off her thinness, her arms and throat an odd unclean dun colour against its yellow; it seemed part of some story of hidden intensity and sexuality. Evelyn and Moira felt an admiration which went beyond envy, they knew they couldn't replicate Doll's high style – and yet the things she said were almost purposefully banal and flat. Words, and for that matter cleverness, were for the common people. Moira swept the drawings together hastily before Doll could look at them, put them away in her portfolio.

Evelyn could see the family resemblance now between Doll and Paul – the deep dropped eyelids, sly smile – although what was ripe and open in his face was narrower and sourer in hers, not exactly pretty, *jolie laide*. Brother and sister both watched Hal, more or less covertly: his assurance attracted them, showing brightly against their opacity. And Podge loved Paul fatally, that was obvious. She allowed herself to touch him whenever she passed him, trailing her hand on his shoulder or in his hair, painted red nails poignant on her blunt fat fingers. Paul didn't mind, he was perfectly kind to Podge and lit her cigarettes, and it was evident that she hoped for nothing from him. In place of her heart's desire she tended to his brother Tommy, tactfully and capably, trying not to remind him that he was an invalid.

*   *   *

After a few drinks, when everyone wanted to dance, Hal and Paul carried in a gramophone from another room and Sinden presided, winding it up and sharpening the needles, choosing what to play. All the records they had were from twenty years ago or more: Ambrose and his Orchestra, Isham Jones's 'Who's Sorry Now', the Old-Time Singers – the awful silly sort of music their parents' generation had listened to. Although the house and everything in it belonged to these young people, they seemed to have no interest in updating it, or choosing their own music. They preferred laughing at everything, holding it all at arms' length, singing along with irony to the old words. *Daisy, Daisy, give me your answer do, I'm half crazy, all for the love of you.*

Evelyn could feel her will dissolving into the martinis she drank, until it hardly mattered any longer that her hair was lank and flat, or that she'd have preferred *Andromaque*. Pressed up against one man after another, she was absorbed in the sounds of their shuffling feet and the scratchy, tinny music, or the logs shifting in the fireplace. Podge and Tommy sat out, smoking on the sofa – Tommy never danced, they said, as if this were purely a matter of choice. None of the dancers made much attempt at conversation, moving together in the lamplit space around the fire, swapping partners by unspoken agreement each time they changed the record. Paul was adept and graceful and Evelyn was aware at close quarters of the sweetness of his body, closed off from her; he and Hal were both fixed now on their drinking, pausing often to refill their glasses. Hal's serge uniform prickled against her face when they danced and she thought he was bored, disappointed with these English people and with his evening – he couldn't even be bothered to choose between Moira and Doll, holding each of them very close in turn, as if he hardly noticed any difference. Dancing with Sinden, Evelyn hid her eyes against his shoulder. For as long as she didn't remember how she disliked him, she could allow the pleasurable sensations that flowed from their limbs moving heavily and even clumsily together. Sinden wasn't a good dancer but he knew what he was doing, all his concentration intent upon her.

Then at some point all four girls were streaming up the broad stone staircase with its crimson carpet and brass stair rods; Podge had said they ought to show their guests around the premises. Sludgy portraits in oil, from the end of the last century, glared down at them out of the half-dark on the landing, only the eyes plainly discernible, and suggestions of rosy flesh on the women's bare shoulders. The girls' own young frivolity and femininity seemed negligible beside the weighty lives that had been lived here. Evelyn said that she and Moira must go home, but in their intoxication now Podge and Doll wouldn't let them go, they needed them, insisted they had to stay the night. The men had settled into their drinking, it was too late, they wouldn't want to get the car out. Podge would telephone their parents for them if they liked, make their excuses. Evelyn protested that she had classes in the morning, but only half-heartedly: she too was caught up by this time in the phantasmagoria of their evening, pushing aside the velvet curtain that hung across an arched entrance, flinging open doors in a long corridor, looking into one empty bedroom after another, shrieking at ghostly furniture draped in white sheets, massive armoires and tallboys, unglinting cheval glasses, glass cases of stuffed birds, wall-mounted trophy oars, shelves of leather-bound uniform volumes. They'd not been in possession of the house for much more than a year, Podge explained, since they'd inherited from their aunt. —It's only ours because our cousins died in the war. Aunt Nancy's sons. I'm Uncle Mottram's sister's daughter, Paul and Doll's father was his brother.

—Our cousins haunt us, naturally, Doll said. —They were such dull good boys.

Extravagantly Podge threw open yet another door.

—You see, we can all sleep here tonight. We can all sleep anywhere we like. I'll lend you my pyjamas, or you could wear Aunt Nancy's nighties. These wardrobes are full of her things, you wouldn't believe it, what an apparatus. Furs and hats and peignoirs and corsets, tippets and galoshes and veils and underbodices.

—We ought to have a great bonfire, Doll suggested.

—On the front lawn.

* * *

In her blurred, numb state as they ran around upstairs and then ran down again, Moira was focussed on the American soldier, who must be made to choose her by the end of the evening. She didn't even like him or find him particularly attractive, and yet she'd invested him with implacable power and set him as a test for herself, win or lose. She was fixated on the sheer oblivious male mass of him – not so much his face as his broad breast, against which she could bury herself. There was nothing to hope for from Paul, and the other two men, depraved and sick, weren't thinkable. Hal was inert, a rock, and what she desired this evening was collision, obliteration; she was dreadfully afraid of failure. Having made a bet with herself – not just for this evening, but for life – on her looks and her wits, she mustn't falter or look down, she had to carry her performance through.

Moira was energetic and dynamic but also anxious, and eaten up sometimes with doubt of herself, fearing that she was guilty and selfish. The throb of disaster and shame seemed always close at hand; she'd been so sure of the trumpet player at Vincent's party, and yet he hadn't telephoned. The news of Robert Cassidy's death had flooded and bewildered her. Was it somehow her fault? The truth was that she'd been relieved to grow out of her feelings for Cass: he had been too impulsive and difficult. Signing up to go to Malaya had been typical of his quixotic, wasteful gestures, just like his inviting Moira to Paris when they hadn't any money, or anything to do there; they wouldn't have lasted a couple of weeks before he was tired of her, moping again over that unattainable girl he'd always wanted, who was so perfectly beautiful and unspoiled, and married to someone else. Moira had been obsessed with that girl for a while. And now she was in competition for the American with Doll, who looked insignificant at first, and yet was subtly advantaged by her class and her worldly experience, her aura of corruption. Moira was fascinated by the other girl's quirky, sexy appeal, the little brooding face, crowded features, big eyes and twisted mouth, figure hunched like a skinny bird of prey. She wanted to discount Doll's odd looks and yet Doll entranced and interested her – more in truth, perhaps, than Hal did. Moira often dwelled in her imagination – with a close attention that was almost yearning, almost generous – on certain other women who were her rivals.

Podge telephoned their parents in Avonmouth: she had exactly the right voice to reassure them. The Bentley had developed a flat tyre, she said, and Paul didn't want to change it in the dark. They would make sure the sisters both got to their classes in the morning. When she came back into the drawing room she was flushed and triumphant like a fibbing school-girl. —So now what shall we do?

There was a danger of things falling flat, once it was definite that the sisters were staying. More drink by itself would only weigh on them and make every-one stupider; when Moira suggested Dare, Truth, Kiss or Promise they grasped at it, although the men claimed they'd never heard of the game before. —So this is what you girls get up to when you're by your-selves, Sinden said. When it was his turn, and he opted for Truth, Evelyn asked him what his first name was: he'd been so secretive about it, when they met him on Saturday. —Oh no, I'm not telling you that, he flatly said, but the others shouted him down, even Tommy, and said he must obey the rules.

—I know what your name is, Tommy said, with an

exulting cruelty in his face, as if they were still boys at school. —I'll tell them if you don't.

—I don't care, Evelyn said hastily, retracting. —I don't mind really if you don't tell.

Sinden was momentarily cornered and resentful, then gave it up with a shrug – a realist, he was quick to abandon any false position. Putting on a comically solemn voice, he said he was called after some silly sod who swam the Hellespont.

—Leander! But it's a rather lovely name!

—Oh Leander! Tommy mimicked. —It's such a lovely name!

—What the hell is the Hellespont, anyway?

A spirit of outrageousness was unleashed. They made Podge dance all by herself to Ambrose's 'Let's Make Love'. —Kissing noises! Make the kissing noises! they insisted. Moira had to climb around the room on the furniture without once touching the floor: she kicked off her shoes and was game, Sinden and Paul helped carry her across some impossible gaps. When it was Hal's turn and he chose Kiss, Sinden said he should kiss Paul, and everyone laughed. —Kiss her instead, Paul said with graceful resignation, gesturing at Moira: possibly he still couldn't think of her name. Hal was fairly drunk, lumbering up from where he was slumped on the sofa and swaying on his feet; Moira braced herself expectantly. His kiss was hungry enough, though impersonal; she tried to convey her readiness subtly, in her response to him. Then Doll dared Paul to dress up as Aunt Nancy, and brother and sister disappeared upstairs together; when they came down again Paul was austere and absurd and unsmiling in a beaded navy crêpe frock, with an ostrich feather in his hair and lipsticked mouth, while Doll was Uncle Mottram, trousers rolled up and wearing an air-raid helmet.

This had to be the climax of their game. They wound up the gramophone again and Paul and Doll foxtrotted together, in their roles as distinguished and elderly; Hal danced with Moira, shambling and heavy against her, murmuring in her ear, wondering where she was going to sleep tonight. It would be too bad, he said, if she slept all alone. Tommy said that his brother disgusted him. And Doll hadn't played the game, he complained; mucking about upstairs with Paul didn't count, she needed to dare something of her own. Doll had taken off the helmet; she was piquant in her voluminous trousers and white shirt and bow tie, with her cigarette in a holder and her hair scraped back, her eyebrows painted thickly in black. When Hal dared her to take off her clothes in front of everyone, she only laughed. —You're so blatant, Hal. I mean, how dare you, really? No beating about the bush. Don't you think you're rather a brute?

—I suppose I am a brute.

—Now you've annoyed her, Paul said lazily, in his aunt's dress.

—She isn't annoyed. She likes brutes.

In the firelit room, without fanfare, as casually as if she were undressing alone for bed, Doll began taking off her clothes: unknotting the bow tie, taking out the collar studs, unbuttoning the shirt and shrugging it off her shoulders, unfastening the belt on Uncle Mottram's trousers and letting them fall around her feet. Underneath she had on only a pair of torn silky knickers with sagging elastic: Moira would have been ashamed to go out in them. Doll dropped those too. Her body was revealed, quick and secretive and animal, unselfconscious – satisfying, like the brown kernel of a nut. The stiff fuzz of her pubic hair was surprising; the small slack breasts with their dark spreading nipples were derisory, insulting. Moira had drawn any number of nudes in her life-drawing classes, and yet she was scalded by Doll's self-exposure, this nakedness not veiled in art or any performance of beauty. The thick-painted eyebrows were preposterous. Swiping up her knickers from the floor, Doll dangled them toward Hal, who snatched at them, grinning; she hung on and wouldn't let go, then began to pull him toward her and out of the room with her, chirruping as if she were coaxing a little dog. —Come along then, silly billy. Come to Dollie. There's a good boy.

Their connection was farcical, Doll's little buttocks childlike from behind, Hal a great bear lumbering after her in his bulky uniform, held by the silken rope of her knickers. When she tugged he might have let go out of sheer callousness: Moira felt the risk the other girl ran. She would have looked an awful fool if he'd not followed her. Probably by now, though, Hal was beyond any preference for either girl, so long as he could find oblivion in one or other of them by the end of the evening. Jocularly Tommy shouted after Doll, calling her a tart, saying she was just like her mother; he seemed agitated and energised for a moment, with more colour in his cheeks. Sinden gave a low appreciative whistle, listening to the two of them processing upstairs: Doll's light voice gloating and teasing, Hal's momentous tread. — Your sister's got style! he said.

—Style! Is that what they call it these days?

—The Yank can't complain about our English hospitality.

The room seemed to lose half its vitality, without Doll and Hal. Paul was suddenly uncomfortable in his dress, and announced he was going to bed. Moira was standing all this while beside the mantelpiece, steadying herself with her hand on the cool stone, which seemed hardly warmed by the fire. In one part of her mind, in her real self, she couldn't care less about Hal, a boorish undistinguished man she hardly knew. And yet because she'd set him up in another part of her mind, to be king for a night, and now she'd lost him, she thought this setback might be fatal. The whole thing came tumbling down on her – Robert Cassidy, Hal, Paul, the trumpet player. Even while she braced herself upright she seemed to be falling through layer after layer of defeat and humiliation, and she felt a surge of hostility against Podge, who was so plain and inept, with failure written on her forehead. —Would you mind showing my sister and I where we're supposed to sleep?

—My sister and *me,* Evelyn whispered, but only to herself.

Podge waved her hand vaguely. —Just take anywhere that isn't occupied. I'll show you the bathroom. Is the party over? Is everyone going to bed?

—I'm going up, Tommy said. —I've had enough. Where's my damn stick?

—Would you like me to come? Podge asked him humbly. —In case you can't sleep. I could read to you.

—For Christ's sake don't fuss, woman.

—Would you like hot milk? Shall I bring you a hot-water bottle?

—Hot-water bottle's not a bad idea. For the pain.

*　*　*

When the others had made their way upstairs, Evelyn seemed to see Sinden, at the other end of the sofa, as

101

if across an infinite distance, blurry; the last logs shifted in the fireplace, it was still raining outside. The quiet in the room was tangible, subtle and tender after all their noise. —They've forgotten about us, Sinden said.

—I need to find where Moira's gone.

He asked her to come to bed with him, as if it was just a joke; she was shocked, and said she couldn't.

—Why not? You're only young once.

—But I don't have any feelings for you.

He hardly seemed interested in that, although he was so absorbed in her, staring at her. —I wish you hadn't cut off your hair, though.

Evelyn stared at him, remembering that her hair needed washing. —Goodness, my hair? I had it cut months ago. Why ever not?

He was very romantic and serious, gesturing something, a swirling movement in the air. —I have this idea of what I'd like to do to you. Gathering up your long hair in my hand and holding it.

She contemplated this, frowning. —I suppose just to yank me around like a caveman.

For a moment he was disappointed in her, spoiling his dream of female loveliness. Then he saw the funny side and they laughed together companionably, which progressed naturally enough into his shuffling along the sofa and sliding his hand onto the back of her neck and kissing her. As long as she kept her eyes closed she could forget that he was NPA and she hated him. His kissing was very skilful; his hand roamed inside her jacket too, and touched her breast through the fabric of her blouse. Because she'd drunk so many martinis – but not too many, just the right amount, she wasn't in any danger of being sick or falling over – the kissing seemed like a thing in itself, very slow and sweet, independent of their personalities or their outward selves. It was the true culmination of their evening. If he'd been a boy of her own age they'd probably have stayed there on the sofa for hours as the room grew cold, necking and working themselves into a state, but Sinden stood up quite soon, and helped her to her feet. She was dizzy from the kissing rather than from the drink. —Evelyn, lovely Evelyn, let's go upstairs.

—Oh no, I don't know.

His voice was slurring and confiding; held closely against him, she was aware of the pores in the oily thick skin of his nose, the gold signet ring on his finger, his consoling smell of cigarettes and cologne. —Paul's very pretty but he's no use to you. You need a real man.

—Do I?

She thought of Donald then, dismissed that thought, and wanted Sinden to be Leander in this moment: she called him by that name, trying to remember whose lover Leander was; not Dido's, because that was

Aeneas. At least she could locate the Hellespont. An impulse of irritation twitched in Sinden's expression and he squeezed her rather hard. —You're a bad girl, aren't you? Worming that name out of me. A girl always wants to find out a man's weak spot.

—That isn't it! It isn't a weak spot.

In that moment anyhow she knew he didn't care what she called him, because he was bent on her – all of his effort was given over to persuading her to submit to what he wanted. Even more than the kissing, this was what seduced Evelyn. It was still a brand-new thing to her, and extraordinary, the way a grown man, with all his power and importance in the outside world, could turn the whole of his attention so completely on a girl like her, whom otherwise he might have despised or discounted. She didn't seriously consider, yet, the question of whether she despised or discounted him. Sinden desired something in her which she hardly even knew that she possessed. Only yesterday she had been an irrelevant child; how amazing to find herself now at life's core, the object of such brusque, blind, heedless, hungry pursuit, as if nothing else in the world mattered.

* * *

He took her upstairs to the room with the trophy oars, inscribed in gold with the names of the crew, which must have belonged to one of the dead cousins, and where Sinden's things – a masculine-looking toilet case, tooth powder, some letters in manila envelopes torn open, a pile of pressed shirts from a laundry, cufflinks – were set out on a boy's desk, stained with ink and scored with a knife. Evelyn thought to ask him then, jolted by the idea, whether he was married.

—Me? Ha! Married? Now she asks!

—But are you?

—Not me, not any more. Once burned, twice shy.

When she confessed to him that she was a virgin, Sinden only marvelled briefly, with a little condescending tenderness. Then he was businesslike, finding a towel to spread underneath her. —Don't want to embarrass the char in the morning, he cheerfully said. Evelyn mostly shut out afterwards what happened next, though not because it was anything horrible exactly: it wasn't horrible. It was only that she couldn't recognise the girl who'd given herself over – and even eagerly, at certain points – to such actions, or at least submissions. It was almost a relief that Sinden was ugly, because of what she'd allowed him to do to her. The kissing downstairs had its aspect as charming, picturesque, if you'd been witness to it: but not this. The memory was a hidden shame, and an excitement. —You like it, don't you, he said, as if he subtly insulted her. And she couldn't help owning up, in the heat of that moment, although she was ashamed to remember it later: yes she did, she liked it. At least she liked it in the early stages. After that there was a little difficulty and pain, as she'd expected, and then it was over fairly quickly – she felt some disappointment. Was that all? And she was conscious of Sinden's withdrawing his interest immediately; his last kiss was perfunctory, before he rolled over to sleep. —Not too bad, was I? he said. —The old chap knows a thing or two.

Still, now she was experienced.

It was only then, when the man lay sleeping beside her, that Evelyn took in the whole new astonishment of her situation. She shifted very slightly away from him in the bed so that no part of her body was touching his, aware of the smell of the skin of his naked back so close beside her, so masculine and alien, an affront in a new language she couldn't yet read. Sinden had turned out the light before they got into bed, but she could just about make out his shape in the bleak large room with its high ceiling, beige blinds drawn down over the windows, those oars like bars across the wallpaper. With her fingers she traced the patterns behind her – fat fruit, a garland of leaves? – in the bed's oak headboard. Could this really be her, lying beside this man on the prickly towel, wetness and soreness between her legs where she'd been used? She had meant to spend the evening reading Racine, at home with her mother and her brother. What had happened instead seemed to have two opposite faces, and she couldn't choose between them. It was a humiliating drunken mistake full of risk, the very thing nice girls were warned against, which would shame her and ruin her forever. But it was also a revelation of lust, savage and real, into which she must pass in order to become an adult, and sophisticated.

* * *

When Evelyn awoke hours later, Sinden was gone and she was glad of it. She saw in the early light what she hadn't noticed the night before, that there was a sink in one corner of the room; when she turned on a tap the pipes gave a juddering noise, so that she shut it off quickly, dreading waking anyone. But she'd saved just about enough cold water to wash her face and between her legs, with a flannel she found in Sinden's toilet case, rinsing out the flannel as carefully as she could afterwards, knowing he'd be offended by her using it. Brightness pressed around the drawn blinds at the windows, and when she lifted one to peek she saw that the world outside was transformed. Brilliant light from a cloudless morning sky, still pink-tinged from dawn, glittered on wet evergreens and frostbitten grass in an extensive garden which seemed an untouched winter paradise. It made what had happened to her seem weightless and easy after all, only part of a new dispensation: everything could be repaired and restored. How their mother would have loved this garden, Evelyn thought, with its crazy-paving paths and arbours, its well-pruned hoary ancient roses grown over love seats, the knarled black branches of its apple trees, its fishpond skimmed with cracked ice like thin glass, and its stone heron, fishing. Everything was clenched in the expectation of spring. Aunt Nancy's gardeners had gone on tending to it, according to her instructions, in her absence.

Inside the room too, when Evelyn dropped the blind, the air was brittle with cold; she put on her clothes quickly. She hid the bloodstained towel, shoving it into the back of a drawer among neatly ordered piles of male woollen underwear and socks, which must have belonged years ago to one of the dead cousins. Then she had to look for Moira: with her shoes in her hand she crept along the corridor, trying to remember which rooms had been empty the night before. At least she found the bathroom, to her relief. She didn't pull the chain after she'd peed, not wanting to make any noise; she was still bloody and sore, and softened a few pieces of toilet paper by rubbing them together, to stuff inside her knickers. In the next room, Paul was asleep and didn't stir, face down among the pillows, muffled under a raspberry silk eiderdown; she closed that door again quietly and then hesitated. Above all, for some reason, she didn't want to violate any invalid vigil of Tommy's, or discover Podge administering hot milk or some other secret solace to her cousin. Instead, when she pushed the next door warily a few inches open, she caught sight of Sinden, also asleep, in one of those rooms where the furniture was shrouded in dust-sheets. He was stretched across a bed which didn't seem to have been made up with sheets at all and was chaotically tangled and rumpled, a thin blanket pulled up across his waist, coverlet wrapped around his chest. Evelyn recognised with a shock of intimacy the scrabble of his wiry dark chest hair; for a fraction of a second Sinden's familiarity, so recently acquired, claimed her. Wasn't he hers? In almost the same second, however, she saw Moira scrambling up out of the blankets where she lay beside him, seemingly wide awake, still wearing her petticoat, her make-up smudged and her hair in her eyes, signalling furiously at Evelyn. —Get out, she hissed. —Go on, get out. But wait for me. Get our coats and wait for me outside.

*   *   *

Waiting outside on the drive in the beautiful frozen morning, holding on to Moira's coat and her port-folio, Evelyn was briefly consumed with rage against her sister. How could she? Why couldn't Evelyn ever have anything all to herself, even Sinden? Why did Moira always have to be first? Or in this case not actually first but last, which was worse. When Moira emerged from the house, she stooped to put on her shoes at the front door, then grabbed her portfolio and threw on her coat while she set out at speed, not stopping to look around her at the weather. Evelyn hurried after her, down the drive which ran in dank shadow between tall conifer hedges; their footsteps crunched on the frosty gravel. —How sick do you feel? Moira said in a furious undertone. —Are you all right?

—Not particularly sick. Come to think of it I don't feel very sick at all, considering.

Moira shuddered. —I feel dreadful. I don't know what's the matter with me. I must be coming down with something. God, that was possibly the worst night of my life so far.

—I never even wanted to be there in the first place. It was all your fault.

—I don't even know where we are. Aren't we miles from anywhere?

When they reached the bottom of the drive, Evelyn thought if they followed the road they would come to the Downs, where they could catch a bus into town. —At least the sun's shining, she said. —Let's go to Carwardine's for coffee and cake.

110

Moira was in quite a state, wiping at her eyes angrily with the back of her hand. Luckily they didn't see anyone, and no cars passed them; the private road was stony and potholed like a country track, its big houses set back out of sight behind walled gardens. A thrush sang in a tree, full-throatedly. —I don't have any money, Moira tearfully protested. —And Carwardine's won't be open yet anyway.

Evelyn reassured her that the café would be open by the time they got there. —We can't just go home or they'll know something's up. And I have a ten-shilling note.

—That horrible, awful man.

—We were so debauched, Moy!

—How could he? Gloating over it too.

—I suppose we'll laugh about it in the years to come.

Fiercely Moira turned on her. —We have to never, ever, mention it. Not to each other, not after today, nor to anyone else, ever. You have to swear, cross your heart, on our mother's life. I really mean it. No one must ever know.

—All right, if you insist. I swear. Though not on Mam's life.

—On the Bible then or something. It was just all an awful mistake. I was feeling so low and I couldn't sleep – there weren't even any sheets on the damn bed. I don't think much of their standards of housekeeping, even if they have got ten bedrooms and a butler.

—The butler wasn't in evidence. I expect he's a drunk too.

—And then *you know who* came along and he was nice to me. The way they are: I expect he was nice to you, too. I didn't realise about you until he told me, and by that time it was too late. Of course he couldn't resist letting me know. Cat who'd got the cream and all that. I suppose he'll tell the others about it.

—He wouldn't tell Tommy, Evelyn said. —That would be too cruel. They're all afraid of Tommy, because he's dying.

—Do you really think he's dying?

—Don't you? I saw it in his face.

Moira said that she hadn't looked at his face, she hadn't wanted to.

—Sinden might tell Hal, Evelyn went on consideringly. —But then Hal will go back to America, so he doesn't matter.

—Makes me sick, so sick.

—What if we ever meet Sinden again though? He'll *know*. Which would be hideous.

—We won't meet him. He doesn't even live in this city. And I'm sure the others loathe him, they're only using him. If ever he crosses my path again and dares to look at me, I'll turn him to stone.

—What if he's made us both pregnant? Would that technically be incest or something?

—Christ, Evelyn. Just don't. He won't have. He wasn't that sort of man: he didn't even *look* fertile. I expect he knew what he was doing. And anyway even if he didn't, and we were, I'd know where to go to take care of it.

Evelyn paused to take that information in, then mused on her own train of thought. —But what if we didn't do that though? And what if we both gave birth to horrid little goggle-eyed babies? Both born on the same day and both looking exactly like Sinden only miniature. Wrapped in identical shawls. One pink, one blue.

—Don't be ridiculous. You're ridiculous. Stop it.

—Leander and Louisa.

Moira couldn't help laughing, because everything was funny, even when it was also desperate.

＊　＊　＊

They weren't even the first customers in Carwardine's. It was quite a walk across the Downs before they reached a bus stop. When eventually the bus came, Moira headed upstairs as she always did, and sat right at the front; beside her Evelyn hung on queasily as they rattled across the open green spaces and then dived downhill on their way into town. Like gods they spied from their altitude on shopkeepers winding out canvas awnings, butchers shouldering carcasses across the pavement, greengrocers setting out crates of cabbages and onions and oranges, housewives wrapped up against the cold, with shopping baskets on their arms as if this were just another ordinary day. Moira confessed to Evelyn that she'd spotted their father on this hill once with his girlfriend, who was polished and tall and elegant; Rose didn't have a chance, they were bound to divorce sooner or later. Evelyn was less afraid of this news, after what had happened last night.

As soon as they arrived at the café they went straight to the Ladies, where Moira splashed water on her face and they combed their hair and put on lipstick. It was too early, thank goodness, for the horrid old woman in there who expected tips. Choosing a table in the café window, they ordered coffee and shared a Chelsea bun. Evelyn persuaded Moira to use the café telephone to call the trumpet player and arrange to meet up with him later; Moira returned from the telephone triumphant, and with the news that his mother cooked breakfast for him every day. This was a revelation: they'd imagined him savagely solitary, even in his own home. It was funny too, because everything was funny. —He'll want you to cook him breakfast then, Evelyn said. —When you're married.

—Under no circumstances will I cook him breakfast.

—You'll have two darling little children and he'll call you Mother.

—I'll look at him blankly if he ever does. *Oh, is your mother here?*

Then when Donald passed the café on his way to classes, they rapped on the window and he came in eagerly to join them; Moira was nicer to him this time, and he said something clever about Matisse. Everything in the sisters' future began unfolding from that morning. They were full of self-doubt, feeling unclean and flawed and conscious of wearing last night's crumpled clothes – but in fact in that moment they appeared just as they most aspired to appear, veiled and opaque and desirable like the mysterious young women in a French film, with hidden lives full of significance and power. Moira wore her coat unbuttoned warily, with its collar up, silk scarf loosened, gold knots of her earrings resplendent against the silk. Evelyn leaned forward with her elbows on the table, talking animatedly, gesturing with her cigarette for emphasis. The outrage of her new experience must be written in her face, she thought, for Donald to read. Sunlight slanted dazzling onto the round glass tabletop and diffused in their cigarette smoke; spoons chinked against the white china cups, as they stirred more sugar into the bitter coffee.

Acknowledgements

Thank you to Hannah Westland, who first suggested a novella – I thought, absolutely not, and then this one fell into my lap and I couldn't not write it. Thank you to Jennifer Barth, always, and to dear Caroline Dawnay and dear Joy Harris; thanks to Deborah Treisman who published the first chapter as a short story in the *New Yorker*, and also to David Milner for his meticulous editing and his trust. Thanks to Gilly for the chemistry.